*Susan,
I present you
dreams. Love,
Geist*

YOU ONLY BEND ONCE
with a *Spoonful of Mercury*

Cover art and interior illustrations: Jennifer Robin

Pretty Stones originally appeared in the following publication:
*Ladybox Zine Series: Even Snowflakes Heal and You Can
Download Skin.*

The fonts: *Garamond Premier Pro* for the body text,
Businessman Light by Vladimir Nikolic for the chapter titles,
and *Intrigue Script* by Mans Greback for "with a Spoonful of
Mercury."

Subjects: LCSH: Surrealism—Fiction. Anthropocene Disaster
Reportage—Fiction. American Celebrities—Fiction.

www.farwestpress.com
First Edition
ISBN 978-1-7365388-8-3
Printed in the United States of America

for you,

child of **FUTURE-PAST**

My dreams are filled with people I could've known or loved who are now OD'd or departed, people I could've had sex with, see-through clothing I could have worn, bars and communes and green rooms and the woods behind the house I grew up in which seemed like woods to me as a child but in reality it was half of an old lady's backyard filled with a rotting wheelbarrow and unkempt maple saplings. In my dreams it feels like finish-line, like paradise, a performance that apparently requires live animal parts and a friend of mine says they can be mailed to her address as her postman is used to handling leaky or decomposing matter, blood-filled packages sealed with Carolingian wax, chestnut leaves...

Oh, is **this** what you're in for?

In dreams I walk with you.

I laugh to myself when I think that I am shoving on the world a detailed chronicle of my pathology, but then I realize—it's your pathology, too. Your *Evil Twins* and *Thumbelinas* and *Jack and the Beanstalk* and wouldn't you like to be a pepper too...your *Bruce Willis,* your *Rocky Balboa,* your alien spacecraft with vivisection under disco lights and the permanent hiss of fog machines. *Rihanna* spits the meaning of life in an indigo bottle of mineral water. *Yoko Ono* in lion-tamer's pantaloons. *Fukushima. Three Mile Island.* Those plastic flossing devices that you never want to use, but your gums have started to bleed and you have to use them or you will be like those toothless mammies and pappies you see drinking at the wooden bar on Burnside, the ones who look like clown paintings.

The New Missiles can reach us in six minutes. Frogs and bees are gone, as if aliens took them, but it was the *PCBs,* or *PFAs,* or pissed-out Prozac, or the stuff that looks like soap bubbles released in a river the Cherokee called *Long Man.* Earbuds, pudding cups, smartphones. The *Rock,* or *Plymouth* Rock? Phil Spector is dead! Jarring scarcity. Everyone loves *e-girls* and *Lil Nas.* Spending five paychecks for Bose speakers in a forest fire; wood witch, you'd better pick up every stitch! Payday loans, hocking a solid gold wedding ring for sixty bucks, but you're evicted anyway.

You see Bin Laden's face on a donut, but you are mistaken. No hot water. There was never hot water. What is hot water?

We are all changelings here: Stolen at birth from a world of trees and streams and placed in a data-creche of heartbreak, told that the way out is to be a *fearless coder* and use a proper eyebrow brush. Steeped we are, in a bath of fetishes and apprehensions, all seven billion of us, yet we carry one ability no matter where we're placed. We were born to do this...

Born to do what? You may ask.
Dream.

In dreams I walk with you.

We wake from living a thousand lifetimes every night. Better worlds than the places we live; worse ones. Our fixations magnified, mangled. When I was a child I was shocked when I would ask adults if they dreamed and they said no. I didn't believe them, about *dreams,* or anything.

In dreams we escape angry men and failed romance and dead-end jobs and the lumps in our necks or guts or souls that we can't afford to have seen.

In dreams, I walk with you.

One night about four years ago I dreamed of a race of six-foot tall beetles who sucked out the contents of human minds, processed them, and shat out transcendence. This beetle excrescence was highly sought-after. One sip and you'd be bodhisattva-level, baby. Beetle-juice is the key to ultimate spiritual ascension.

In dreams, time moves faster. A year can pass in three minutes. We have *cortical flow:* all regions of the brain, even the disused ones, awake and radiate the names of first-grade teachers, Rick James, islands on ancient maps and birdsong, turning them into the **NEW.** We feel impossible sensations, slipping like ghosts in and out of strangers' chests—we are endowed with wings and fiery spines. We hoard to our heart's content, then realize that we can't carry all of those purple velvet boots and boxes of cheesecake into waking life. Take these! Doom crystals, or maybe a collagen-boosting soporific.

> *To dream a man carries a falcon on his fist and speaks with it signifies honor. A woman dreaming of soiled napkins foretells that humiliating affairs will thrust themselves upon her.*

Those bits are from a *dream dictionary.* Remember those?

Someone in the playground was bound to have one, palm-sized and usually held by the girl in a huddle by the far wall of trees who would show us, the misfits, the ones with too-thick glasses and werewolf teeth, how she could foretell the future.

It runs in her family. Now she has a book.

She would open the slim volume (with a green or purple cover—featuring a mystic image like an eye or a heart or brooding psychedelic sea) and we, quaking for acceptance, the backs of our knees sweaty, would try to remember our *best* dreams to tell her, the ones that featured nudity or flight instead of the ones where we lost the ability to read in the middle of a test.

In my dreams, there is an apocalypse. After a certain age I realized that there is *always* an apocalypse—but it's *fun!*

I am homeless. I am free in a way I don't feel in waking life. I roam through a hugely depopulated world, where survivors live in a network of underground tunnels, repurposed hospitals, shopping malls and art galleries.

I find myself spying on egregiously wealthy men and women who hoard brie wheels, conspicuously amoral scientists, rock stars rumored to be Satanists and Libertarians. I am free but I am also hungry, so I try to scavenge or steal or charm my way into a series of Cadillacs and blinged-out panic rooms.

If I have to blame any cultural factors for the content of my dreams, I'd point my finger at nuclear stockpiles, dystopian cinema; a childhood reamed with reports about global warming and how our nation is overtaken by a corporate cabal who directs endless waves of meat to invade resource-rich nations, because *someone's* gotta sell guns and planes and powdered milk, and our wages don't rise, and we are helpless, but at least we have Four Loco and eight-dollar cans of nacho cheese.

Two of my best woman friends *also* dream of apocalypse. They are both six feet tall and weigh nearly twice of me and know how to put men in headlocks (and they probably could improvise an effective *Vulcan Death Grip,* if they had to) and while they are more suited than I to survive a global-scale disaster (I am 108 pounds and virtually blind without corrective lenses) all three of us dream about civilization cracking all the same.

One of them—the platinum-blonde Valkyrie one—believes that we, through our circumnavigations and battles in these dreams, have been rehearsing for our starring roles on the stage of cataclysmic change for decades—yes, as soon as our child-minds cottoned onto the direness of the *Sixth Great Extinction Event.*

In dreams I am a nomad, only occasionally meeting people I've met or loved or hated in *real life*. My exodus bones lead me through mazes of future-past, a thousand-thousand almost-nows. I've tried to map these dream geographies, but no matter *where* I roam, the location eventually turns into my childhood bedroom or backyard in Syracuse, New York.

My mother and grandmother loom as if on puppet strings. My dead grandfather appears with part of his skull missing, but doesn't seem to notice.

I follow a witch and her companion to a pink quartz rock formation in the desert, because she knows a way to survive the hurricane that will sweep away our twenty-first century erections; it will sweep away everything.

Of course there is a price.

What do your exodus bones tell *you?*

I remember a period of my early twenties when I was a speed freak, well sort of. I was hooked on family-sized bottles of *CVS pseudoephedrine* marketed as nasal decongestants. I wanted to transcend language—really transcend *any* sequence of linear symbols—get past this tacky film of humanness, the brain's processing limitations, its defined "five senses," the emotional bias, the *collateral mortal shebang.*

I'd end up nodding off on someone's sofa after having been awake for three days and abruptly wake from 45-minute nightmares involving demons and thousands of voices trying to speak at the same time. I was hooked into an intergalactic switchboard, heard what all lifeforms talk about: No matter what dimension they wafted on, it was all about medications and bosses and moisturizer.

I'd solemnly intone: *What are you? Show yourself!* after feeling a seemingly omnipotent presence that had leapt from the tail of my dream to the foot of my bed.

I quit the uppers, but kept my last jumbo-size bottle, traveled with it from Rochester, New York, to Portland, Oregon. Five years later I threw it at the barred window of a basement jock after breaking up (for the hundredth time) with a 20-year-old man who worked in a porn store and wrote acid poetry and hung out with Portland's version of a racist Johnny Cash.

Many a time since then I wished for my bottle back, because it was still half full, and ephedrine went illegal without a script.

So *that's* my way of seducing you. Now, *did* I?

In the following slim volume, you will see a fraction of my inventory of dreams, a crass dose of pure, pulsating pop selected *for entertainment purposes only.*

Do you feel it? I'm holding your hand.

Yes, I'm a loner. I know you're a loner, too. But let's *pretend:*

I am holding your hand. Come with me. Look! There's a mirror, many mirrors. *They* are watching us, but we don't have to care!

This night belongs to us. This *infinity.*
Come!

...World!

Just *watch* us...
...as we prowl the arcades of fallen memory...

P.S.: If you encounter a figure in the following dreams whose name or relevance you don't recognize, feel free to consult the Glossary (a.k.a. ***Jennifer Robin's Pop-Cultural Decoder***) on page 112.

MY BEST FRIEND

Last night I dreamed about Marilyn Monroe, and she was magical.

You see, she was a tomboy and a gadabout. She had a special warmth, not unlike a campfire. You would want to be near her and bask in her glow. You felt privileged to get to see her, be accepted by her.

We were on a cruise ship that was also a Catholic church. A film was being made, but true to the rumors, Marilyn, while starring in the film, was often too distracted by sex, drugs and rock and roll to be able to do much acting in it. She would spend long hours in a powdery sun-up sleeping off the previous night's accumulated toxins. She would be passed out in overalls, like a factory worker—overalls and vomit-stained high-top sneakers. Her sleeves were rolled up; a baseball cap was firmly affixed to her head, even in sleep.

She woke up with a rosy glow and started roaming the cruise-ship-church for more buddies to elbow and caress. I was her roommate and I felt a duty to find her when the directors were frazzled and red and needed her to complete a scene.

I would shake her sleep-shoulders and follow her up and down the maze-like passageways of the cruise-ship church. When she was lost, I would find her, and her pale white pigtails and shiny cheeks would make me feel like melting, that someone so beautiful and masterful of...well everything, so it felt, was happy to see *me!*

When we got near groups of people, like this group of punks selling purple hair dye out of a glass case in a beat up cloudy-sky parking lot, I'd watch her work her wonders, watch her drift from me and entertain the masses.

They would do anything for her, because her smile made them feel important. I wanted to be like her, and with her, and perhaps I would never grow up. Perhaps I was permanently a teen looking up to my best friend, *Marilyn Monroe.*

He was a young alcoholic poet who always wore a cab-driver's cap, and his work was freeverse, eclectic, and ultimately so frivolous (mixing war scenes with disinfected toilet bowls and goldfish) that no one understood the hidden profundity between his lines, if there was any.

Underneath his baggy free-box clothes his body was surprisingly muscular, like that of a rock-climber in a place like Colorado, Arizona, all of the mystic basins to which these Peter Pans go.

I saw his body because the poet was naked in a bathroom, and a woman he had a crush on, one of those impossible gorgeous Italian women who has hair like velvet ink and a body like a tongue depressor, she was stripping, getting naked.

He got naked too. They were in a shared bathroom which may have been in a dorm, or a hotel, or some ultra-modern communal living situation where people pay to live in condo-coffins for sums that would feed a village in Peru for ten years.

So both of them were naked. She giggled. She scampered to the toilet where she let out an electric yellow stream. She flushed and jumped back in a demure way, to lean on the edge of the sink and yes, talk to the guy.

They hadn't touched yet. This was just the beginning.

So the poet gets the idea, being that his crush just relieved herself in front of him, that he can do the same—so he sits down on the toilet.

You heard me; he sat down. He even let out a comment about how he could feel "the turtle's head," or that the horses were charging through the gate.

I strain to remember properly and think he said something about a raging bull—and it raged, it plopped out so dense and heavy that there was very little air exposure.

His turd raced right into the water with minimal

smell—but it was still *too much!*

The woman who was, two seconds ago, thinking of kissing him, started glaring at him. Her nakedness now looked cold, as cold as a porcelain sink, as cold as a bus shelter's metal anti-homelessness bench in the shape of a waffle iron on a snowy December morn.

My dream changed scenes. I was coming from a show and sitting on the steps of a massive brick apartment building. It was ornate, institutional, with a wide stone stairway, young city-people coming and going, powered by the illusion that their lives were headed somewhere.

I had a scanning device on me that gave me the name of the driver in every car that went down the street. I heard a loud blast of music and a convertible went by. The scanner told me that the car was owned by a heavy metal star, well-known to be a Libertarian.

The moral of this dream is look before you plop.

CARNIVAL

She did burlesque performances in a traveling circus. She drank heavily and she wore silver shoes and her hair was dyed doll-blonde so that she would shine like the moon in eternal spotlight. Decades were passing, but she had a baby who was always a baby in a crib, a fetal-alcohol-thing that never seemed to grow larger or move or ask for milk or food or flesh at all. The clock tolled 1969 and the baby died while the woman pranced under spotlights.

The world was changing and people no longer paid a traveling circus for marvels, for death-defying feats. The nightly news delivered gore in the comfort of any home. Assassinations, riots in the streets, rock bands where men became women and women had navels and nipples and made the noises of full-color orgasm.

When the baby died there was a calm in the air. The baby was quiet anyway, but now the baby became trash, became something to be disposed of before time made the body fall apart.

It was always afternoon. It was always night. It was always dawn. It was always a shopping mall where high school girls bought space suits, and I had a wad of cash in my pocket, thinking, I could buy the space suits too, but they are made in China, made to fall apart, like time makes bodies fall apart.

A woman was in love with a man who kept on changing size. In some moments he was six feet tall, and in other moments, six inches. Was he an alien? Was he cursed? Was this natural? All the woman knew was that he was the only man on this Earth she had met with this ability. He was a janitor in a labyrinthine apartment building—it stretched on in an elaborate French Gothic style with buttresses, octagonal rooms, vaulted ceilings, forking corridors, inexplicable classrooms with inkwells and parachutes attached to the ceilings. Oh yeah! And the constant hornet buzz of ceiling-mounted fluorescent lights! It was an apocalyptic age; at any moment there might be the explosion of mortar shells, the shouts of invading armies, the groping for poison capsules, the constancy of loose stools, the sudden realization that one's ambitions will never be realized, not with this blood leaking from one's guts. But we who lived here, who haunted this world—a *world* with more gravity than its *inhabitants*—we took it in stride. We took our being feather-light in a world of metallic shadows and shrugged our shoulders and dubbed it forever.

So the woman who dated the man of ever-changing size was feeling HOT for him. She felt like electric velvet, knotted, clenching, sliding against itself, ecstasy a luxury within her reach as she skipped playfully to the places her lover would usually be, and couldn't find him, and finally she came upon it—in a boiler room, behind a door mounted in the middle of a wall—riveted steel, meter-maid, milk capsules, mashing time.

She opened the door and saw the miniature bathroom, its tiny fluorescent lights on, and the shower, still damp, a bathtub only four inches long, and the arms and hips of the naked man who had slipped in the shower and was now as pale as the porcelain tub, dumbed by death, indigo bruises blooming on his arms and thigh. He was dead and she wailed and picked up his body between two fingers and she felt as if a flash flood had taken away her mind, her forehead throbbed, and her body turned into a monster made of kelp and clamped on the knowledge that she would never have such a lover again.

MORRISON GROUPIE DEATHWATCH

It *was* Jim Morrison, and he was dying. Instead of the bloated found-in-a-bathub opiate-fiend we have been given in reality, he was the leonine sex-glossed cherub of the first singles, the hollows of his cheeks as deep as riverbeds, his pupils wide, turned to rims of black holes, pregnant with a permanent unknown that our telescopes itch to probe.

Jim was thin and sweaty and unconscious. Due to the publicity his presence would draw, he had been moved to a remote hospice run by a bunch of shady doctors who reminded me of high school principals.

In milky daylight they crowded around his bed. I was with a gaggle of Jim's favorite groupies, high-level groupies who were treated like his next-of-kin. We leaned close to Jim's statuesque form and as we did I noted the sculptural quality of five transparent tubes hooked up to his neck, right below his chin. Instead of medical devices these tubes looked more like antennae, or the wisps of an old Asian monk's beard as rendered by a thick and impressionistic brush. They were like straws extracting the milk that Jim was made of; the pearl dew of the ancient Bacchanal.

Jim's breathing was shallow, but steady. Watching his body inflate and deflate with each intake was a hypnotic experience. I think any of us could have sat there and done so for hours. The doctors told us they were going to do some routine maintenance on Jim and that we should leave the room while they did.

When we came back, the straws were removed from his chin, gently dangling inches from his flesh, and his breathing had stopped.

We knew he was dead, and the doctors had done it. They had made the decision to remove all that was Morrison from this world. They had taken away decades, perhaps even half a century more of what he could create and feel. Now he was a statue, a dead statue, ever so briefly containing a cosmos of dying cells that could have continued the Jim.

So there you go—*Jim*. And I love the Doors, but I'm not a Doors *fanatic*. I haven't even thought about the Doors for a while, other than a T-shirt I bought when I was twelve that said: "Jim Morrison, American Poet."

I thought the sentiment was so corny that I didn't even wear it back *then*. But you know, Jim *was* a poet, and he probably dies a million deaths in people's dreams every single day.

I was living in a warehouse after the disaster had taken place. It was a restaurant, a hospital, a distillery, a blacksmith's, a death parlor—whatever we, the survivors, needed it to be. I was in a room with green walls and bookshelves and a crow flew in, looked into my eyes as if addressing me, and tipped over, dying immediately. I picked up its body, still not believing it could so suddenly be gone. It was sleek, and young, and healthy, and when it died its eyes remained open, black as a moon's dream of night, clouded, yet still seeming to see.

I put it on a shelf with some books. It lay there, sideways, staring yet not staring at me.

The room I was in was a managerial office. A server came in with glittering hazel eyes, an apron, no time for random aberrations like a crow in a gust of distracted wind. We knew each other, but she had no time.

I told her I didn't know what to do about the crow. The daylight was going and at night, we the people did not go outside.

"Just keep it on the shelf. The air is so dry in here. It won't rot overnight."

Then a crowd of people gathered, including James Spader who was arrested by the sight of a dead crow on a shelf, so shiny and stuck between states.

Spader puffed his chest, like a king of crows, he expanded in his suit like an old rubber hot water bag. A voice both mellifluous and outraged issued from him:

"We cannot, we absolutely cannot leave this beautiful beast on a shelf. It must be afforded a proper burial right away. We ride now in my car to celebrate and memorialize its life in nature."

Not many people had working cars, but it was no surprise that Spader had one squirreled away in a bunker made of black quartz and brine.

Oh, where would we fly in the night with the husk

of a crow, so lifelike, its eyes never turning away, reflecting everything, including what we most try to hide? The list grows longer by the minute...

I now pronounce us *Scar* and *Scar*.

THE FIANCEE

In my dream I had a severely broken jaw and I was pregnant and Howard Stern was going to marry me.

In my conscious life I have never had sexual fantasies about Howard Stern, and I've only listened to his show twice. I recently saw a picture of Howard Stern in a tabloid, married (I think) to someone, and suspiciously—as in surgically—as youthful as ever, like a skeleton covered in smooth and ebullient taffy.

Hey, this is my subconscious mind and that is all there is *to* it.

This is how it happened:

I was living in a dormitory. It was night. It was always night. I may have been hungry; I may have been doing laundry. Howard Stern started hanging around the hallway, and I entered a room where he was.

My dream-friends were horrified. They didn't want me talking to someone as politically incorrect as Stern. My next-door neighbor got jealous and excited because this was HOWARD STERN. He was gay and attracted to Howard and wanted Howard *all to himself.* He told Howard all sorts of lies about me, that I was stupid and covered with warts and had bad breath and I don't know what else but for some reason Howard still came back and talked to me, and then the *accident* happened.

My chin was busted open. It was crushed to a pulp like a soggy Easter egg.

Did I break my chin in a room of vending machines? Running on a grassy field? All I know is that suddenly there was a lot of *air* down there, and blood was rushing out and I knew the spot needed to be closed so my entire *brain* wouldn't leak out, so I wouldn't lose the air in my lungs.

I was given emergency medical treatment and a promise from Howard (you see he was a surgeon, too!) that he would be the aesthetic *Maestro* to restore my jaw to its former dimensions. *(Surgeon and shock-jock...*that should be a sit-com.)

I couldn't believe it! Howard was still interested in me even when I resembled a trash-compacted rat.

"Actually...it will be an easy fix," he pronounced. But there was one condition I had to adhere to. My jaw had to mend in its mangled and *uncorrected* state before I could have the artistry of Howard's scalpel applied to it.

As I convalesced, not seeing Howard, lying around in bandages, I became obsessed with celebrities with broken jaws or other sorts of legitimate facial injuries (I mean facial injuries that were not fictitious excuses to get elective plastic surgery). I watched a Youtube video of a blonde actress with elfin features who was making a "letter" for her fans to show how much she loved them, even as her face was horribly disfigured. She had a hole in her cheek the size of a silver dollar, but for the video she had shaved off a speck of soap to fill in the hole so she wouldn't frighten anyone.

So this is where I was at: Howard Stern was my boyfriend and he was sending me love letters, but I didn't physically see him anymore. It turned out I was pregnant.

One would assume it was by Stern, but he was never around, so it would have to have been an immaculate conception because he hadn't visited me in the flesh for *months*. During this time, I had a sense of expectation, like a teenaged girl wondering what it would be like for our love to be 'consummated.'

Howard sent me a letter saying that because of the pregnancy he'd bite the bullet and marry me. *Hell,* he'd simply marry me because *thoughts of this made him happy.*

Several weeks passed. I was at a new medical facility. My bandages were taken off.

Before a mirror I assessed my partially missing jaw: My reflection told me that I would have to get used to people giving me a wide berth in supermarkets and uttering things like, "Awww, that's too bad, that's really a shame," but I could *do* it.

I said out loud to my grandmother (who is dead), or someone like her:

"I could go *on* like this. I am passable. This will *do.*"

My treatment was moved to South America. I don't know which country; one of the many sunny countries with palm trees that a white American thinks of at the mention of the words, "South America." I was driving or being driven through a resort town, high plateaus and fleshy green foliage on hair-covered trees; bodegas glowing in midday sun.

I was in a special medical facility which Stern was supposed to visit when he was ready to do the surgery. It seemed that I had been waiting a long time now for Stern to come and do the surgery.

Rather than feeling medical, my quarters were in a small stucco inn—clean, with personalized familial charms. I showed one of Stern's letters to a male nurse attending my jaw.

The nurse confirmed what I could already sense from the letters: Howard at *one* point may have had a crush on me, but it had long since passed. I may have flattered myself that he had a deeper interest in my personality, *anything* more than my looks—but now he had cold feet and was yet compelled to continue writing these letters, promising to do my chin surgery and marry me. His heart clearly wasn't in these feeble lines.

My savvy male nurse looked at me like "Oh, HONEY," but thought better of saying more. He smiled and pushed out the sentiment that yeah, Howard *seems* like a *nice guy,* but I could tell what the nurse was thinking.

Then I looked at Facebook, at what I thought were Stern's *public* declarations of love. I realized that these declarations were on a super-private setting that only I could see. I had always wondered why none of his Facebook 'friends' wanted to become *my* friends, why not even *one* observer commented on his declarations...and now it was clear as day: No one saw this fiction other than

23

me!

I felt a sense of relief. I was not attached to someone who treated me like a flower that must be watered every other day.

I was in a South American town, in a car going up a steep hill. At the bottom of the hill, it was hot. At the top, snowflakes were falling.

I wanted to turn around, go back down the hill and out of this arctic hell, but the traffic was so thick and I was locked in.

FUNERAL MUSIC

I love you. I listen to your funeral music with wild abandon. I am in a library that is covered in dark maroon oriental rugs and draperies. A college-aged girl is here with me. We lean toward a copper chalice full of drugged toffees. We chew them. We go through the stages of a psychedelic trip. It is brief, each stage. We feel elation, arousal, out of our bodies and back. We are embracing, laughing in our grubby library clothes. It is over quickly. There is no shame here. Others approach to do the same.

There is Seattle, temples, a mother commissions an eight-hundred-dollar dress for a child and keeps the tab open. There are zombies. You work hard to book a venue and arrange a video shoot for your favorite musicians. This absorbs months of your life, your paper-doll energy. It is 1996 again and I select a transparent plastic shoe to wear at a fashion show. I am discovered by wealthy patrons. I'm the next Kate Moss; lollipop-eyed Little Miss No Name.

Telescopes work hard to find you. I relax. There is nothing to attend to but the feeling of slow, inevitable motion. No emotions need be grabbed at, wallowed in, indulged. I am hungry, but I am free.

The woman is blonde and looks about fifty years old, her body losing fat, cheeks sinking yet still moisturized by a regimen of products scented tea-rose and neroli, and daily mists of an indoor humidifier. Her apartment is small and her job is clerical. Every day she sifts through medical insurance claims in order to discover redundancies and incorrect billing procedures. At night she sinks into lucid dreams that take place in a desert landscape. She does not recall having limbs or a face in these places. The buildings look like tombs, and her being sings with the sensation of sun. She wonders if in these dreams she exists as a form of conscious light.

When she was younger she won a huge sum of money from a class-action suit, so much money that her friends called her the "heiress," but it's all gone now.

When she was young and rich she crossed paths with a man who was an artist. Sometimes he called himself a writer and sometimes he was a comedian and other times he simply billed himself as "The Scourge." He had problems with self-esteem, so many that even at times when he developed a large fan base and had pitches from magazines and gatekeepers of *Face* he would enter the familiar embrace of pills and graveyard hours and leave the cities he lived in to play invisible on farms and in attics of people who grew sick of him before he even arrived.

But like a cat, or garnished credit card debt, he came back. He survived longer than anyone expected him to, and his voice grew stronger.

It is a speakeasy in a Victorian house and the times have grown gray. People are gray, wear gray, speak gray, entomb sentiments in plastic bags, stored for later. Specimen gray is the lifestyle.

In this gray time the woman enters the speakeasy at midnight and lingers until dawn. In an upstairs room she meets the writer. He is tending bar. This is an accident.

She feels very close to him. Her mind is festooned with tenderness. She hasn't seen this man in twenty years!

I was supposed to be with you. She nearly speaks the words while thinking back to when they were young and the world was purple and orange along with gray.

I had money to be your agent and give you your own TV show. I could have guaranteed you a spotlight at any time of day and we would've made love, so much love that we would force the spotlights to wait until we scraped off days of sweat and chalk and milk and jism and drool and hair from our bodies, purified by instinct.

This image flashes through the woman's mind while a group of people in black robes and hoods enter the room and put her in a noose. The writer behind the bar has a heart attack.

She is hung, beheaded, roasted on a spit, and restored to life to walk through the next room of the Victorian house to see her next death.

It is an open air market in Marrakech. It is a swamp in Georgia, an alley in Camden Town, Jerusalem, a box car, a hoax.

She sees her many deaths and the man's many deaths, and after each one they are returned to the house. These do not feel to her like lucid dreams. Someone outside of her body is controlling this stage, this show.

PILGRIMAGE

Many speculated that the mad scientist was an alien. Intellectuals made pilgrimages to the perimeter of his workshop where they would burn fingers and noses and fry to death on an invisible electric forcefield. You could see boxes, barrels, a storage room on the other side. Littered on the ground were sacrificial piles of belongings: sleeping bags, clothing, cosmetics, coats, framed photos, hastily removed underwear and socks left in crooked balls. I could visualize the moment when each pilgrim was filled with a holy understanding: You must leap through the forcefield **NAKED!** Pure! Some traveled months to find this parking lot and meet the alien on the other side. They believed that no one else on Earth could help them.

Next to me a blanket was on the ground. A man had stacked the remains of his life with a clinical eye for detail. He had been a professor. He left proof of his identification, a stuffed animal, a cigar box, two diaries.

I must read those diaries! I thought to myself. *They may tell me what led him here, what this place is.*

A group of pilgrims surrounded me. One of them threw a bird against the forcefield and we listened to its agonized squawk as it fizzled to death.

Someone had the idea that if we all held hands, the volume of our connected bodies would absorb the electricity and we would be safer than going through the forcefield one at a time. I caved in to the sweaty grip of palms on either side of me.

We got so close to the forcefield that I could feel the hairs stand on my skin. The blood under my scalp jogged strangely. The line of bodies were tugging me closer and I wondered if we would make it through...

THE WEDDING PARTY, AN ENVELOPE OF SAND:

The coroner's room is set up like an 80's nightclub, bodies cleansed to the point of being plasticine, hanging at evenly spaced intervals from the ceiling. The dead are dry, turned to art, lit by blue neon which spans the floor of the room. I enter with a reporter. The coroner smiles and offers us drinks. He has an affable Polish face, a wide jaw and hungry blue eyes, a shock of blonde hair that stands on his head like the crest of a tropical bird.

I am at a wedding party when Neil Young sends me an envelope of sand. He is living with his parents, or grandparents, in a small New Mexico town. We had fallen in love the summer earlier. He wants me to know that he hasn't forgotten me. Although the envelope was mailed from New Mexico, it has air mail stamps and mysterious markings, as if it has passed over oceans, and through an additional dimension—forty years of time—in the span of two days.

The wedding party is in a green land: Maples and oaks grow near a massive lake, far from desert clarity. I carefully rip the edge of the envelope to open it. I peer at the sand inside, trying not to spill it, lose a single grain. I grind the powder between my fingertips. Mixed in with the sand is a strip of paper with a sentence type-written on it. Is it a fortune, a poem, a message about escape velocity?

The wedding party's house is surrounded by trees. A humid wind makes the trees touch themselves. The sound of leaf on leaf is an ever-present music that lulls visitors into premature sleep. To stay awake, the guests start drinking.

Patsy and Edina set up a vintage store in one of the rooms of the house. They think of me as a nuisance. When I go to refresh my drink and turn around, their racks of clothes, their lounge chairs, their bodies—have vanished.

The wedding house has an emergency room. Patients are brought in on stretchers, survivors of car crashes, gunshots, domestic disputes; freak accidents where someone's hand goes in a blender but the person is sheepish about relating how this came to be.

One housewife walks around with a knife that fell onto her skull from a freak cooking accident. It is sticking out of her pate, the soft zone where supplicants from the Older World get trepanned. Because of the angle of entry, because of the brain not having pain receptors as the rest of the body does, she walks around, unaware that a stainless steel butter knife is lodged handle-deep in the seat of her consciousness.

Shirley won't leave Laverne alone. Her amorous advances are growing to a fever pitch. Laverne feels horrible about this, telling Shirley that she wishes she swung THAT way, but she just doesn't. Laverne is wondering if she could at least try, try to run her hands over Shirley's breasts, as white and firm as sugar cubes.

They have this conversation twenty times a day, as the wedding party grows more complicated, unravels before our eyes.

Last night I dreamed that I adopted a goat that turned into a man. At first it was a small white goat with a trim white beard curled into a ball on my chest. Next it was six feet tall and walking on its hind legs and wearing plaid sportswear.

I felt I had to break it off with the goat and started lecturing it tersely on the responsibilities of clothing and feeding it, and he reacted badly by throwing himself out a window, a mess of teeth and blood.

LEGENDARY DRUGS, 1973

An old woman lived in a warehouse in New York City. She made snuff art, or at least people thought she did. Crates of carefully arranged ropes, duct tape and bloody blankets would be displayed in her rooms and left out by the garbage cans, like Cornell Boxes of murder, however no body parts were found. One day she threw a grand party, which David Bowie and Iggy Pop were going to attend.

I could feel it in the quality of air; the noises on the street: The year was 1973. People emerged from cabs and private cars in excited huddles, draped in their finest silks, sequins and furs, platform heels wet with melted snow, hair styled to resemble lemon sorbet, and they would disappear on the other side of the blue enameled door that advertised the Lady's ground floor gallery.

There were drugs, legendary drugs. The woman was giving out a bomb of acid and smack to select guests. These gifts were wrapped in blood-stained cotton and bits of confetti, and carefully dismembered shreds of garbage bags.

David and Iggy were late to the party. The street traffic was dead and no one appeared to be home. They entered the empty warehouse, terror dancing in their guts. The hostess might appear with a hatchet and put an end to their ambulatory dreams, but they found nothing and went back outside.

A rumor had spread that guests had bad reactions to the Lady's gifts and as a result she had ended the party early and thrown the remainder of her drug-bombs in the garbage.

So David and Iggy commenced their search. Knee-deep in the dumpster, they grabbed all of the bloodstained tissues and blankets and wads of tape they could find, hands diving and sifting through soft, damp, fruit-smelling piles, and loaded the best-looking selections into the back seat of a car.

They took turns on the highway, sifting through the garbage, desperate for a unique high.

"Fuck, it's only *art!"* Iggy yelled, as David steadied the wheel, eyes bloodshot, the sun not so much rising as cringing behind oily-looking clouds on the horizon.

He let the woman's wads of artfully-stained cotton and dismembered stuffed animals tumble from his palms.

And they drove, and they drove into the morning. It felt like they had been awake for a thousand years.

YOUR BODY IS A GOURD AND A NEST

Your body is a gourd and a nest.
This is the story of the *butler's daughter...*

The butler serves in the house of his aunt, who is of a higher class. The aunt has pity on the man, allows his wife and children to live in the extra rooms of her house, the constant thump of child-feet running up and down stairwells, the crashing of silverware on bumpy, glazed porcelain from Leicester, marbles the color of fish eyes rolling incongruously on uneven boards before a fireplace.

Afternoons find the girls singing under gables. In winter, the sashes are sealed and the butler uses a bellows for the fire, rushes back and forth with hot water bottles for his aunt's arthritic feet. Her cheeks are firm and full of life; her smile is high; but in limb she is quickly turning to an albino crow. Her body is a gourd and a nest.

She is a widow. The man knows this to be: When his aunt dies, her brother will claim the house, dispense with hangers-on. The butler and his wife will be penniless, homeless, hoping to marry their two girls to whatever men of comparable class will take them and as soon as possible.

The saplings at the edge of the field grow taller and the oldest daughter watches her sister change: The wee one with one dimple and two natures falls into trances, gets sick, more than a child with sunrise in her cheeks ought. It is said that when she was born, a comet raced past the moon—was it a comet of great light, or great shadow?

It is 1850, or 1882, or maybe even 1794. Minstrels cross the countryside singing for supper with mandolins; tinkers nod down every block for tin scraps, coal chunks, alms and pastry. Locusts and flocks of partridges blot out light, lure the human brain to prayer. In petticoats a woman fetching herbs by a river can slide into the water and die of hypothermia in three minutes. One kiss can lead to syphilis, triplets, a name like *witch*.

The butler's wife cooks chicken hearts in May butter

34

and sorrel, pours beer brewed with *myrica gale*. Holidays come and go, and the youngest daughter, sometimes sickly, sometimes proud and running in the sun, finds her legs yearning to run *further*. She's been bleeding for three years and her legs want to outrun the heaviness that pulses so strong in her loins.

A black swamp beats in her, churning for release. Her womb is a gourd and a nest.

She runs to the end of the aunt's property and enters the forest. She weaves through a stand of alder until she reaches a clearing where the stump of an old oak lies fractured on the ground. She hears the music of a man nearby; but he is not a man; he is a boy, and it isn't a music she hears; it's the dancing of his legs, a shimmy of his arms.

He is wrapped in the thinnest silver scarves like a fairy shroud. He has turned into a mist that is condensing on her cheeks, her neck, moving under a cloth that feels too heavy, too human on her chest.

When she returns to the house, her clothes torn, her body full of music, she doesn't understand the alarm in her mother's voice or the rage in her older sister's eyes. She has scratches on her cheeks and wrists but doesn't notice. She is drowning in a milky rheum of music which she hopes will never end.

Even as her mother hastily inspects her arms and legs and instructs her to change into sleeping linens, even as her body feels like ice under her sister's palm, she is planning how she can escape and dance again with the one who is living mist.

She sleeps for two days. She is unaware of the changes. She needs to *drown* in him. To drown is to be preserved, as if in sugar, in linden blossoms, in a fog that feels like a thousand fingers and a thousand tongues. Her body feels so heavy, a gourd and a nest, but she longs to become bone, and then as bone subsist with mist.

Within the year, her older sister is engaged. After a long day of rehearsals for the wedding, the church is locked and empty.

At night, the girl sneaks in. As if she is a bride herself, she sways down the aisle between stoic wooden pews, pews that she imagines in their hardness yearn to paddle flesh.

An illicit music fills the air. *He* coalesces; dancing about her; his skin sometimes silver, sometimes green, sometimes red, sometimes ebony. He is music, he is ice. She is fire, and she is smoke. Her body begins to writhe in her nightgown, no bloomers, a moisture dripping down her thighs. She feels her body opening for him and growing tight.

This is dancing; this is ecstasy. She pulls the gown off her shoulders. She is naked. The faces of parishioners flicker in and out of space before her eyes, as her nakedness gleams before them. But it is night; they aren't *really* there. But what *is* time? Who cares! The man who is mist, who is music, envelops her and enters her completely.

Some would say she is infected. Some would say she is enchanted. Her body is behaving in ways that no longer look human. Her skin moults—fine, translucent flakes that fall from her cheeks like fly wings. She can sleep for up to a week, during which time more than a faint cast of frost appears on her eyebrows. Frost-color strands appear on her scalp, cracks in a dark and sweat-filled mane. Thick black hair grows on the tops of her feet. A substance like cobwebs issues from her face.

While her body is asleep to the humans, her *essence* is running in a forest. She is searching for him, not finding him. Her mind can *feel* him there. Where is he? Is he with other, fresher ladies? Does he only love them before they are infected? Surely he could not love her now, now that all she does is *sleep*?

Her ribcage is so heavy, but her blood is filled with liquid dawn. Her blood is Venus squatting on the horizon. Her blood is a sharp intake of breath before orgasm.

Her body ages, and her family has no choice but to

move on, accept a daughter who is condemned to *endless sleep,* however with the combined finances of her great-aunt and her sister's in-laws, a last attempt is made to save the butler's daughter from ruin:

A grand carriage is constructed that is meant to keep the sleeping woman isolated—not just from other humans, but out of a more *unspecified* harm's way.

It is a round wicker cage built on rolling stilts. It uncannily resembles a bird's nest, and teeters fifteen feet off the ground. Instead of being carried by horses, an ingenious system of pulleys are maneuvered by a Ladyservant who is hired to accompany the sleeping woman at all times, and on occasion pour liquids into the comatose mouth, wipe debris from the face, now looking bruised and wasted, covered as it is in cobwebs and iridescent scales. The Ladyservant must climb up and down a ladder to use any facilities on the ground that her body requires, as well as fetching supplies for her Ward.

One spring afternoon, the sort of glistening hour when a body's lungs are nearly incapacitated with growing green, the Ladyservant and her sleeping Ward have wheeled into the forest. The Ladyservant simply can't handle being cooped in the house any longer with this *monster.*

They move on a winding dirt path, and boughs of trees brush against the elevated nest. The Ladyservant releases her hold on the pulleys and climbs down the ladder to gather something which she knows to be in a hut.

An old woman sells fruitcakes here. Or fortunes, or other notions. The servant is only gone a minute, but once gone, the girl immediately wakes. The girl can sense him— yes, *him,* the devilish, dapper creature down there, luring her to *come* to him, open her body to him.

In one fluid lunge, as if she is dancing through the sky, she rolls over the edge of the carriage and falls fifteen feet to the ground.

Her bones are not broken. They are not able to break. She starts to dance, swiveling in the direction where she feels him to be, but his location shifts rapidly; is he behind this or *that* tree?

The Ladyservant returns and is terrified. The Ladyservant looks and looks again, hoping her eyes are deceiving her. The girl is nowhere to be found.

The girl, or what is left of her, is twenty-five-thousand feet off the ground. She is moved through the airspace above upstate New York, headed to what the Agency hopes is a final destination. She is kept in a case in a back chamber of the plane, hooked up to various machines, under supervision from the most recent in a series of jaded scientists.

The subject is isolated from the pilot. His radio is loud. An agent is telling the ones on the ground that this leg of the mission is a success. The body is installed on the plane, but it has had its neck removed by a firing squad.

He repeats: "Yes. We removed its neck with a firing squad, but it is *still alive*."

The Agency is sick of studying it, even possessing it. The Agency conducts increasingly sadistic laboratory experiments, no longer considering the subject a being with agency at this point in its (can they even *use* the word?) lifespan.

What seemed like a gift is now a curse: No matter what you *take* from it, it respires; it sleeps. It not only defies logic; it defies *Earthly science*. And they still can't figure out how to duplicate what it is made of in a way that would say, prolong a president's life.

There have been many guardians over the years—a monastery, a circus, a wealthy eccentric. During World War Two it was stolen by the French Resistance.

I hear thoughts inside the thing they transport. It forms sentences! A mind pulses in there yet!

I am on the plane, and I am near her, or I *am* her.

We feel: *I cannot escape now, and I am afraid.*

GRAVITY, MOTHS, FLAMES:

The Newspaper Mogul was taking me on a trip, and I was trying to keep track of the bags I had packed. I don't know why I accepted his invitation, this man who was known to shift elections, cause oceans to boil, brains to shrink, while jails and landfills and drug cartels grew larger than forests. What did he want from me? He had everything. I had nothing but my lungs.

I got in his slick black rental car and we tooled slowly through a section of a city that was lined with endless expensive 'artisan-made' food stalls, lit up in strings of carnival lights. We were headed to an airport, which turned into the nursery of a hospital sealed from us by a thick glass window. My very first boyfriend, done up in motorcycle gear, appeared to me at different ages, sometimes a boy, sometimes a teenager, sometimes a grown man, cackling wildly and slamming his head into the pane of glass. This didn't appear to harm him, and seemed to be meant as a form of communication.

I was able to leave this institution and found myself walking through my childhood backyard where a pale and unhealthy-looking gaggle of middle-aged nerds were playing raunchy party games, sucking down cocktails like hummingbirds siphoning dewdrops from a daffodil's stamen.

I hovered at the edge of this nervous clump of people. Almost every one of the women had dyed-red 'vixen' hair and almost every man wore some type of monocle or bolo tie. One woman, who was the ringleader, rolled a die or spun a bottle and instructed us, as a group, to strip off one clothing item.

"SHED!" She cried.

Most of us were fully clothed. People began tossing small items, like their shoes, into the center of the ring. Never resisting a chance to get naked, I took off my shoes, as well, and wondered how far things would go.

The woman who was in charge of the game sent a man and woman into the center of the ring, where they were supposed to make out wildly, dry-hump each other as we watched. The two began doing this.

They looked like an accountant and a schoolteacher. They were fully-clothed, mechanical. It appeared as if I was watching two plastic-wrapped pieces of dry-cleaning trying to reproduce, no matter how furious the grinds became.

Then the ringleader pointed at me and a twenty-something hipster-man to do the same thing.

We approached the center of the circle. The man was very shy; he looked like a miniature Mike Nesmith. He had chestnut hair and sideburns and absurdly small wire-frame glasses, and he was dressed in an overly formal way, sealed into a suede-and-paisley vest in the sweltering summer heat. He was very uncomfortable with this whole thing.

I was instructed to lie on my back and he was supposed to do a simulated grind on me. I put my hand on his waist and gave him a look of mercy, trying to let him know with my eyes that he didn't have to worry about offending me, and that I wanted him to know he was with a 'friend.' He gave me a very fast, dry peck on the cheek, and the ringleader told us we could stop.

We adjourned to a small patio area where h'ors deuvres and cheaply-produced poetry chapbooks were being served. I tried to engage the shy hipster-man with eye contact and let him know that we could both 'move on' after the unusual game, but he was still too nervous to look at me.

I was back in the hospital, and it was about to lose its power. There was a massive room of generators, which sat on shelves like aisles in a library, and a man in blue overalls with a mullet, a Polish jaw, and twinkling wolf-eyes went up and down the aisles monitoring their loads.

One of the generators blew up and this caused a power surge that spread down the line to the other aisles of generators. I could see the cascade effect happening and knew that the technician was a goner. In slow motion I watched as aisle after aisle of machinery started combusting.

I ran from this chamber and found myself in dim polished hallways that led to operating theatres and recovery rooms. Their lights were going off. I entered a room where brain transplants were taking place. People were getting all sorts of severe operations that aren't elective in our waking reality, like amputations of the soul, and tongue exchanges.

I found a frightened young woman with cancer who didn't know what to do in the blackout. She moved along the walls like a stray kitten. I put my arm around her and led her to a lower floor.

The lower floor was on a separate power grid, and everything was running smoothly. The girl and I entered in an operating theatre with dim lights and balcony seating, several rows where students and other spectators could learn from the intricate origamies of tissue and vein that took place within.

The master of ceremonies was a sadistic surgeon whom I could overhear making fun of his patients and humanity at large in a cold and precise voice. I caught his eye and the effect was withering. Despite his veneer, I approached him, feeling that I had to tell him the power had gone out on the floor above, and fires were raging.

As I told him this, a dark glow suffused him. While he didn't necessarily like me, he wanted to know *more* of what I was telling him.

He wanted to see how bad the destruction was. I could see the delight growing in him. Soon it would not be contained.

His delight fascinated me. I offered to go upstairs with him, and watch him watch people suffer, even if it meant leaving the cancer patient behind.

Even as I heard the words coming out of my mouth, I realized that I was making an ethically *gray* decision, that it spoke about something in me, something that leans toward the 'dark side,' whatever we take that to mean.

Does this mean I would join Charles Manson or Elizabeth Báthory on a spaceship to Alpha Centauri because their madness would provide a *wilder roller coaster ride* than the regularity of self-sacrifice that comes from helping the ailing and the meek?

(Would accompanying a cult leader or a blood-drinking aristocrat on a space voyage of indefinite duration really be *without* a soul-crushing degree of self-sacrifice?)

There is a nuclear war; a very thorough nuclear war where it seems that every armament on the planet is detonated.

The human race sends up a shuttle carrying a mild-mannered and balding dentist and a little girl who is not unlike Wednesday Addams with a precocious cast to her eyes. For all they know they are the only two humans who have survived.

The Two Surviving Humans hover in a void of space, staring down at their planet, a planet changing before their eyes, with plumes of light and abrupt shifts to the weather patterns as the endless detonations take their toll.

Defying logic, defying physics, the girl and man return to the surface of our planet, where time passes.

There are green spaces which are not blanketed by the debris of nuclear winter. There is a totalitarian state where people are attempting to live an illusion, that the twenty-first century has *had* no war, there is *not* an invading army or a surveillance regime. We are *not* being watched remotely, calibrated and tweaked like a cat cleans its vibrissae in anticipation of tender prey.

The dentist is in a long room filled with molds of patients' teeth, and something is going very wrong. He can sense it in his *own* teeth, in the follicles of his scalp. It feels like a sting operation is taking place on the nature of human consciousness; a sting operation is taking place on sanity.

A PERSONAL MESSAGE

I moved into an apartment in a decaying building, halls lit by bare bulbs. Zombies carried my boxes.

The building was decaying and simultaneously shifting its dimensions: Stairways would come and go, covered in concrete dust and wood splinters.

I was walking down one of the halls—it felt like I was trying to emerge from a cave—when I heard the mew of a cat, saw a flash of Siamese-colored fur.

It was a kitten. I tried to coax it from the shadows, and when it emerged, I saw that it didn't see me, only smelled me, and rubbed against my palm because it had no eyes, or even the flaps where eyes should be.

It quickly attached to me, and I found myself feeling simultaneously smitten and diseased by touching this creature covered in sores, its proboscis growing larger every second until what I was petting was an oversized rat.

I made my way to an airplane hangar filled with Christmas decorations. I asked Bob Dylan to record something with me and he refused, but in a personal message.

The performer is a banquet of steaming macaroni, rice, and saag paneer. The buffet has no power to tell you what you are hungry for. You must be guided by your instincts, whether the fruit-whip Jello or the seeded naan is what makes you whole.

I'm attending a party in a mansion where a sad blonde teenaged girl lives. Her parents are artists, famous ones, and their party has attracted a rare breed of celebrities and avant-garde personalities who make money from what they do. They arrive in iridescent scales and rainbow hanggliders fused to their backs and headgear that makes Marie Antoinette look like a *pill,* but the girl is sullen and wishes she had someone at the party her age who wasn't coated in shellack while containing sawdust.

It is daylight still. The party started early. The girl's parents are in a huddle, having a conversation they weren't planning to have in front of their guests. But it has happened. They are relieved. They are asking their guests how to break it to the girl the way the facts of life work, even though it is the future and everyone knows the facts of life, especially a girl about to turn eighteen.

An increasing number of party guests join in the conversation, nibbling too many hors d'oeuvres for their wardrobe comfort and no longer caring how drunk they get on violet elixirs, egg froth crusted on their lips.

Should we do *books?* Should we do *poetry?* Should we hire a concubine? Perhaps the concubine is safest and would imprint a sense of intimacy vital for satisfaction in future erotic events?

What they don't understand is that the girl has had lovers for years. At this very moment she is inching towards a window three stories high to a ledge where one of the party guests, a woman dressed in a zoot suit with square shoulders and lavender-white hair brilliantined so candy-hard is smiling at her, taking her hand.

The two adjourn to the girl's bed. The girl has never seen this guest before. Her need to be devoured by this woman in the suit is immediate.

Downstairs David Duchovny is on camera demonstrating a routine from his early years in porn.

He whips out his cock from a pair of khaki Dockers and it is partially erect yet hangs to his knee.

The guests are shocked at its length, its narrowness. Women can't help but stare and they find him attractive, in a circus-sideshow way.

They are having a hard time reconciling the fantasies they used to have with the fantasies this knee-length cock demands they construct. Some laugh, some stare with their jaws open.

It could never fit....it wouldn't even fit in a Christmas stocking! It wouldn't even fit in a golf caddy! They don't even understand how it sat so innocently in his pants all those years without looking conspicuous.

David Duchovny is slapping his leg-long cock against a man dressed in a chicken costume, and a live gorilla wearing a tutu.

A party guest in a cheerleading outfit runs up to him and hides behind the gorilla. She plays "peekaboo, I see you!" with Duchovny's cock.

Outside this party, the world is poor, the world is made of green ravines, neighborhoods overgrown with crabapple trees. Puddles line the streets. People have dwindled. The Earth has grown strange.

A mother drives her kids in a car. They live in this car. It is cramped. They handwash their clothes and plates and utensils in this car and there are hooks and bars and the smell of mold all over with half dry underwear and hats and stolen food.

She has somewhere to get fast and drives off the freeway. Cars are backed up, too slow. She must drive in the swampy ditch beside the freeway, and up a hill where a shed with an oven stands.

Next to the oven a gangster is tied to a chair with his bottom half growing small like an ice cream cone, almost sawed off. His chest has slugs but this woman has worked as a nurse.

She removes them, though I don't know why. It seems the man has been left for dead but she has chosen to revive him.

His bloody slugs rest in a tin basin. The blood looks black around each bullet.

The sky is pregnant. The earth is pregnant. Who is spared before we go in this direction? The body is tenacious. It takes a tenacious will to destroy it. Death is a *cause célèbre.*

It used to be one would have to wrestle, run, use a spear. Guns make us small, guns strip our names. Guns make us easy to extinguish.

"I killed you. I'm sorry."

If you forgive people too quickly it paves the way for you to be crushed and willfully crush yourself into moldy cracker boxes for life.

Do you hear it? The noise before you're extinguished, forever.

We do this as a trance, generate noise to blot out the largeness of everything else, the sheer weight of unknowns.

ALTERATIONS

I acquired a suit a man was murdered in (plus his false leg) and a pair of gloves a serial killer wore in a separate incident. I stuffed them in a closet, thinking they'd be useful to me in the future, and they transformed—the suit and the gloves, into two large gray cats.

One cat acted like a casual cat, but the other was possessive and would kill anyone who got too close to me. I could feel murder in the shapeshifter's body, yet his fur was so soft, his love was so strong. He playfully circled around my leg wherever I walked in this world of endless night and bridges rising and falling to let tugboats and navy carriers pass on waters tainted with spent uranium and Celexa piss.

Like a living being, the murder-cat had to sleep, and when he did, he turned back into the bloodstained suit.

I was walking on a bridge with an elaborate shopping structure built on top featuring specialty stores and a parking garage. Most of the stores were closed for the night, except for a fetish-gear outlet and a dry cleaner.

I was walking with a man who was a friend of a friend, and I had never figured out if he was straight or gay. He was good-looking, but had enormous snaggle-teeth that altered the way he spoke. These teeth gave an air of childlike innocence to whatever he said or did—which I gathered was not much. He had a way of disappearing into statistics about sports and the gross national product of Cambodia, despite dressing like Percy Bysshe Shelley.

I convinced this man to take the bloodstained suit, a situation complicated by the man not wanting the jacket, or the dead man's false leg.

He only wanted the pants.

We walked into the dry cleaner's on the bridge. I watched Shelley hand the pants to the man behind the counter. Why doesn't he snag the *chicks,* or *guys,* or whoever he's trying to snag? I thought to myself, as Shelley's graceful hands pointed to the crotch of the pants, and his Dionysian lips explained that he was missing a penis so he'd need the garment altered to precise dimensions for a comfortable fit.

LIVESTOCK IN DISGUISE

In my dream a cow wearing a brown shoulder-length wig, a floral blouse, and polyester pants was slowly walking on its hind legs up a marble staircase of a department store to the shoe department, and I was certain that the cow would be discovered as "livestock in disguise" and not allowed to try on shoes; however by the time the cow reached the second floor she had fully transformed into a human being with wine-colored skin, an opaque gaze, mingling gaily with other shoppers and salespeople, and only the faintest wrinkles around her eyes when she smiled had a quality that revealed her bovine past.

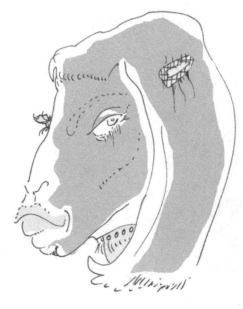

It is considered a breakthrough to enter the lair of the German Scientist. In the future we live in shopping malls which are connected by supply tunnels, concrete hissing with steam-heat that makes a body break sweat like fast food plastic, soul buoyed in ice, made profane in the act of melting.

After passing through a number of stores, dim spotlights, customers nearly gone, I go up a stairway. My guide nods that I may enter the room.

The room is filled with sculptures. Each sculpture is made of dead human bodies. They are coated in resin, dismembered, recomposed. Nerves, tendons, desiccated organs are exposed. Some of the bodies still have flesh on their faces, making them more expressive, tenuous in identity, frozen in transition. They appear to be speaking to me.

The Scientist has countertops cluttered with tools to perfect his creations. Rather than a gallery, this feels like a workshop. The air is filled with the scents of dry rot, formaldehyde, a sweetness that reminds me of wood pulp, very old library books.

I travel through the mall. I am in a toy store. The combined scents of rubber, plastics off-gassing their natures like vengeful lovers, and artificial grape flavorings surround me. This is paradise! Like *IKEA*, like *Forever-Twenty-One*. We are forever fourteen, yet to be siphoned, partitioned, sown.

A group of forty-something men and women are debating politics, something significant that is about to happen outside of the mall civilization.

My high school boyfriend rides a motorcycle. The world has been depopulated, and we are two of the last. A woman who claims to have been in a church choir with my pubescent self tells me a longwinded story about how one of my high school bullies was told she cannot wear dangling earrings.

Our bodies are getting older, but our minds are going backwards. I caress the exposed flesh in an experimental way and enter the second laboratory.

The German Scientist has a *copycat*. The dead in this room are less than a foot tall. Instead of being displayed on stands, they are kept in trays. Each body is a mixture of bird and reptile parts, with incongruous human hands and faces that are sometimes fused, but in miniature.

Shrunken human heads, fingers that resemble the talons of crows; these specimens have sat on their trays for so long that they appear to be covered in a fine layer of dust, mildew, feathers, as if they are moulting. My task is to run wet sponges over the specimens, so that they can be removed from the trays, reanimated.

Are these beings in limbo, invisibly alive?

I wet each body, finesse the brittle limbs so that they won't break off, resemble mummy-dust.

This room is dark, but outside the sun beats heavily, as if I am safe in a year like nineteen eighty-two.

MILK BOTTLE DREAM

This is the earliest dream I ever remember having.

Being raised by one's grandparents means that certain conventional ideas of their generation were not the norm to my contemporaries. For example, I slept in a baby's crib when I entered kindergarten. This crib was kept in my mother's room, and I would be lying in it, drifting off to sleep while hearing the bings, bangs, moans, and roars of the teevee down the hall through the open door. By keeping this door ajar, my mother and grandmother were given the sense that they were supervising me.

My mother's room was painted the same pale, almost-orchid shade of pink it had been since she was a teenager. I would watch the shadows grow as the sun set in the window behind my crib-head, and visuals, often of country drives or vistas from made-for-teevee movies, filled by head. At night, when the room was dark, my mother turned on a small lamp with a fabric shade that would interact with the pink of the walls and illuminate a tall bottle of French perfume she had brought back from Paris a few years before.

This perfume: It was some kind of pop-youth scent. The bottle was a cylinder with embossed watercolor flowers on the glass. The liquid inside was dyed aqua. It smelled like a high sweet lavender. As a toddler it was the most magical scent I'd experienced.

I felt ceremonial about the rare occasions when my mother would let me sniff the liquid in this bottle, until it was all used up.

But anyway, the *dream:*

I was lying in my crib. I could hear the teevee on down the hall, and the lamp was on. I saw a large glass bottle of milk at the edge of my mother's Sears Roebuck ivory-color French Provencal vanity, in the place where the lavender perfume used to be.

I started rising from the bed. I was levitating. *Slowly,*

as if I was filled with helium, *slowly,* as if I was a miniature airship, I hovered closer to the glass jar of milk.

I felt an impulse to connect to this bottle. It was in my hands, one with my face. I was drinking from it and there seemed to be a never-ending supply of milk. I was able, in my periphery, to see my stomach engorged with the milk. I was floating in the air and ballooning out further as the milk supply added to my girth. I bulged so much, and the milk wasn't stopping and I was afraid I was going to explode...

STAND-IN GRANDMOTHER

I had come from the outdoors, bright white light devoid of color or scent. I went down to the basement of my grandparents' house and into the bathroom next to the garage—cobwebs, blooms of pink mold, walls of yellow paint. A short fluorescent tube over the mirror, like a torch of a malignant past, buzzed madly, outside of any sense of night or day.

My grandmother (who is dead) was approaching me. She spoke very few words. What I remember most are the creases of her eyes. She was caressing my arms, holding my hands.

I recognized that she was supposed to be dead, yet I was filled with the immediacy of her presence. When this stand-in grandmother embraced me, her grip was firm like my real grandmother's, and for a moment I relaxed into the ferocity of her nearness, her chest.

In real life my grandmother had very firm hugs. My family had madness, *sure,* but all of the madness seemed to fall away when she surrounded me with her embrace.

I was wary of the dream-grandmother's embrace. My spirit fluttered under it, at once elated, and then confused.

I had returned to the house from a strenuous activity—running a marathon, or hiking a great distance. Stand-in Grandmother seemed intent that I drink enough water to replace the fluids that my body had lost outside.

While in her embrace I watched her examine my eyes. She patted my wrists and pinched my fingers, and I had the feeling she was checking for the volume to return to my blood. She was waiting for the right time to sink her teeth in and *drink.*

This woman was a vampire wearing the mask of my grandmother. I allowed this knowledge to fill my body, while not changing my posture—a prisoner in her buzzard arms, a prisoner of her skin.

WRANGLER JACKET, PURE SAVAGERY

I have arrived in the Hawaiian Islands. A photographer strikes up a conversation with me and decides to marry me. The sun on the buildings is bright and the photographer's cameras bang at his sides like a family of starving children begging for his attention, his touch.

I have no desire to be married and yet I am followed, not only by the photographer, but by a small woman in a Wrangler denim jacket. She appears to come from the year 1975, with long uncombed hair and tight jeans and stoned eyes, as if she has stumbled out of a middle-school bathroom where girls have huddled over a bong made from a Pepsi can. At moments the clouds fade from her eyes and a look of pure savagery hits me, and I am aware she has a hunger I cannot feed.

I am in a park and walk around a row of modern sculptures. One looks like a stack of fifteen mattresses piled on top of each other and covered in liquid chrome. I am wondering if the girl in the Wrangler jacket will stop following me, if she is a human being or some kind of mental projection like the dulpas Buddhist monks spoke of long ago, ghostly thoughts turned into human forms, which once summoned would follow you to different cities, even overseas.

The photographer has gone away, and I enter the mansion of a Hollywood film producer. He is lounging on a round sofa, and the French woman is in his bed. I sense that they have had a relationship for a long time but it is not necessarily physical.

He is scooping generous spoonfuls of Nutella into his mouth. The room smells ionized, the curtains partially drawn. The furniture and carpets are a custard color and the sun is beginning to set.

The girl in the Wrangler jacket has followed me into the film producer's kitchen. She lingers in the hallway outside of his bedroom, blending with the shadows as if to say All of What You Take for Granted is a trick of the light.

The French woman rolls in clean linen, reads a gossip magazine. Her mannerisms are eternally thirteen.

We are safe here. Nothing can go wrong here.

The man and woman start asking each other who this girl in the Wrangler jacket is, who *let* her in, why doesn't she speak?

I want to stay, yet I sense this is an opportunity. Perhaps the girl in the Wrangler jacket who blends with the shadows will attach to the couple and I can escape, escape to the sunset where more ghosts prowl, where it feels like everyone is a ghost struggling for a body, a burden, a catch.

The woman was a rich drug addict and also an exhibitionist. She rented a storefront in a dying mall to live in, where she would be watched by passersby every day like a zoo animal. Chrome racks were affixed to the walls from the previous business, and she hung a motley collection of vintage clothing on them.

The day came when she OD'd on pills and was taken away. I snuck inside the storefront and found hundreds of her pills fallen all over the beige carpet, which I picked up, thinking I could identify them and use them later.

In another part of the mall there was a neonatal ward and an orphanage. I followed a social worker to a farm where one of the orphans was to be adopted. I was walking down a steep and grassy hill and saw a family of mostly boys who were bullies and had red hair. I wondered what traps the red-haired bullies were going to set for me.

When I returned to the city, I was pregnant. I was a gothic witch. A web-cam was installed in my small apartment, walls painted black, spells tattooed on my flesh. Viewers, many of them men who thought themselves to be dark in various occult fashions, wanted to see me cut deeper, cut until I could turn my skin inside out, perhaps unfurl it like a cape that could cover the buildings on the block with a spray of fat globules and poetic viscera.

My mother wanted the child.

My boyfriend who had goat-feet returned. I hated him, and yet his scent was irresistible. I   cradled   Syd Barrett's head in a box, like a living thing. The dimensions of the box were elongated, and his head was somewhat shrunken to fit inside, though his features remained youthful and beatific. In this sense, he could serve several generations of supplicants to come, not unlike a reliquary of a saint.

I did not want to surrender my box to any being. I could sense that Syd's head was communicating with me, so long as I held the box, pacing, ceaselessly pacing, remaining in motion until the soles of my shoes grew as fine as the silk on a Chinese fan.

UNWISE BLOOD:

It started in an old, high-ceilinged room in London, furnished with wicker chairs and regal velvet pillows, and a lanky blonde woman who sometimes sat like a sphinx and departed like a shadow. A number of older married couples were going to a dinner party in this lofty space. Most of the lights in the room were off, and it felt like the guests were arriving after standard dinner hours.

The men and women were drunk, overweight, desperate—the clothing they had pressed their bodies in was tasteful and expensive, and yet gaudy, ill-fitting, like candy wrappers on rutting pigs. They were trying to show off their looks to partners who had long since lost interest, yet perhaps these wrappers and perfumes could pique the curiosity of other lonely guests.

"A last cosmetic bloom before the real decay sets in," I said to myself while realizing I was in danger.

Some of the couples were descending to a basement where the housekeeper, a woman as small as a child, had been placed inside an ornate limestone coffin. The guests were torturing her. I could see blood begin to leak out of the sides of the limestone coffin—stone walls to mask blood, which do not.

The aristocracy were vampires. No drop of blood would be wasted in this ceremony.

A doctor in a blue sharkskin suit and a wild falling-apart pompadour took interest in me. I realized that I was lost and broke and needed to escape the party. He was hailing a taxi, and I ended up tied in rope and attached to the doctor as he began to shake like a madman and the cab sailed into endless winter night, me listening to his laughter while staring at the dandruff on his suit.

Time passed. I worked in a hospital. I was not trained as a nurse, but it was my job to be a high-tech janitor, constantly cleaning and re-arranging the bedclothes, machines, canisters of hygienic swabs, wires and devices arrayed in a modern emergency room.

Doctors would come and go, and seem to lean over the operating table, yet there were never any patients on it, and never any blood or other grisly substances for me to siphon, wipe, or clean.

It was as if the doctors were performing the pantomime of medical care, or operating on invisible patients.

Invisible patients leak invisible blood. Perhaps invisible patients don't have any blood at all.

The operating room connected to a maze of office cubicles and dingy yet comfortable rooms that made a never-ending hive of church basement—a honeycomb made of a thousand church basements, each one covered in wall-to-wall carpeting, linoleum; cabinets of simulated maple and the ever-present hum of fluorescent light that deletes night and day.

A concert was taking place in one of the rooms. I realized that it was sold out and I was the main attraction. I thought of what an accomplishment this was, that I had a sold-out show, but I never ended up performing, as I got lost deeper in the mazes of the hospital made of church basements, waiting rooms, laboratories with unlocked doors.

I broke through the maze of rooms and sun fell on me. It was a cold winter day yet the sun, where it hit my skin, was very warm. I was being followed by a middle-aged man in a bowtie. His eager eyes were enlarged, made babyish by the lenses of wire-framed spectacles.

His bald spot glistened in the sun. He thought himself as a journalist but he was a hired voice. His job was to read weather reports on an AM radio station.

I was lonely, and appreciated the weatherman striding behind me on a path that led from the hospital and deeper into a park, the winter grass grown yellow—or was the grass yellow because of *summer* sun?

The air was so warm and I felt so free and young and

alive that I waved my arms in the air, and took off my shirt, feeling the saliva in my mouth, my heartbeat hasten—I felt the thrill of going topless.

The sensation of showing the world my breasts while feeling so alone and yet so free and alive was overpowering.

I would take off all of my clothes! I did, and climbed into the branches of a tree with very dark bark—a tree with bark as dark as charcoal.

The weatherman was no longer behind me. I climbed higher into the tree, balancing on a branch twice the size of my waist, and yet for such a thick branch, it seemed to wiggle in the air like taffy. I was afraid it might snap, or droop so much that I would fall to the earth and break my neck...

MAGNETIC MAN:

I feel this and refuse to go back to the world of human definitions.

It was the late sixties. I was wearing a white satin bodysuit, cat whiskers painted on my face.

I entered a ranch house. A number of shy boys in dashikis and headbands were trying to impress girls in miniskirts who would one day marry them and have four children each. A man came in from the street and instead of looking like a teenaged hopeful, he was older and there was a raggedness about his clothes. He could have come from the Spanish wilderness four-hundred years ago, or he could have served in the Pony Express. His hair was greasy, eyes wild. His face was ugly until he shoved his features into a smile.

He could be a hippie and the boys tried to talk about music with him, but I could tell he scared them. They wanted to put him away on a shelf but they could not get rid of him because he was carrying with him the power of the outside, the danger, the cosmos. I sat holding the hands of two men who were not preachers but the preaching was in their blood. I got up and followed the ragged man, always staying behind him in the crowd so that I could watch him before he focused attention on me.

The ragged man fell down a flight of stairs and everyone was afraid when he came up the stairs that he might kill someone because in his eyes there was the wildness of a killer. Everyone was secretly expecting it, that he would bash their heads or pull out a knife and give the women cesareans and from each woman-womb would come a true self or a pile of steaming waste and it would be a test wouldn't it, if he was magic or if any of us were magic, if we could taste deliverance?

The boys and the magnetic man began to play music. They failed once, started drifting away from their instruments. The second time I joined them and began to sing. The magnetic man turned to me and said, "You have a good voice."

I had *imprinted*. When the boys walked away my ears were ringing and the rings were in a pattern, becoming a song that made me feel youth and freedom and ecstasy. I leaned my head back on a piano, knowing what I was doing. The stranger who could be a killer approached me and said, *"Do you hear that music?"*

He said his ears were ringing too. No one else in the room in polka dots and rainbows and ribbons heard the music. It had a power. It made one feel fully alive. I looked at him and said *yes.*

Alice Cooper locked me in a sex dungeon with twenty-five locks on the door and three futon mattresses that were as long as the room, which was as wide as a warehouse, and mirrors covering every wall. He took me to a mattress and embraced me, both of us remaining fully clothed. I sensed an interrogation was going to begin, and I woke up.

When I drifted back to sleep again the plot had continued. I was in a cult of Alice devotees who wandered the streets bedraggled, barefoot, and The Great One would arrange secret meetings with us on park benches. He would grace us incognito, his head capped with a blond wig, his body in the costume of a street mime.

I continued to deteriorate in this reality. My life became a Hammer film: I was chained to a street pole by a leash and with a flash of light I was transported from the dimension where I was one of Alice's Slaves to *Our Reality*.

My chains were broken. I walked proudly down the street in hot pants and a blouse tied at my waist, barefoot and covered in dirt, into the heart of downtown Los Angeles.

I got on the talk show circuit, somewhat embarrassed but earning a living by giving repeat performances of my time in the Alice Cult.

In the final scene I am in a wooden-beam brew pub trying to look like it came from Britain three centuries ago and a number of sloppy-drunk housewives are buying me shots in exchange for personal details about being in the Alice Cult.

ELMER ELLERY

He was in love with the woman from afar. He lived in an alien dimension and the mail from the alien dimension worked, yet slowly. One day the woman received an angry note from the man, calling off his crush because she had never responded to his gifts, but the truth is, they had not arrived yet.

How the crush started was *this:* She was in front of her childhood house during an apocalypse, because those happen every day. It was a rather bucolic apocalypse. The temperature was like a dolphin that nudges gently against a hand.

He appeared, and how he looked is not important. To be honest he was half-invisible, so if questioned on how he looked, the woman would not be able to say. He held her hand and showed her how to spit galaxies, slide down hospital halls, and in general he made her feel that she was part of an intergalactic plot, because she was. Technology was more advanced in the alien dimension, and if she had chosen to marry him, she would be tied, deeply, to a plotline where the excitement of spitting galaxies would wear thin.

I mean, *look* at this! He was already mad because his mail had not arrived yet.

When the boxes finally did arrive, all five of them, of varying sizes, addressed to *Elmer Ellery,* she was surprised to discover that her name was Elmer Ellery, but why not? She had just met an alien from another dimension that can only be reached by standing at a precise spot on a lawn near her grandparents' driveway.

She opened the boxes addressed to Elmer Ellery and found books, pencils, mysterious comestibles such as those smoked meats in *Hickory Farms* Christmas packs, and drawings and poems made by the man, but by far the most unusual item looked like a butter cookie with one drop of raspberry jelly in its center.

The minute the wrapping was removed from the cookie, its appearance began to change. The pad of jelly in the center hardened and deflated. As she examined the package, she realized that the object that looked like a butter cookie was meant to *preserve* the jelly in the center, which was the man's sperm. She was supposed to put this inside her body and be wed to him in a *permanent* way.

Scientists and curious onlookers closed in on the box to examine it with her. A woman reporter decided to grab the cookie and do an undercover story on the alien dimension by speaking to its royal family with a claim that SHE got pregnant with the butter cookie, just to see what would happen.

And meanwhile Elmer Ellery watched and pondered the peculiar and frivolous melancholy that comes with a romance that never really is. How can two people, after only meeting for an hour or so and spitting galaxies together be sure that they are destined to spend a *life* together?

Crushes are real, but what they are based on is slippery.

A crush is like a prayer. And yet when an alien cancels a crush because the interdimensional mail took overly long to be delivered, a sadness results, an emptiness results, and a *relief.*

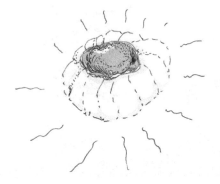

MAXWELL HOUSE INTERNATIONAL FRENCH VANILLA POWDERED COFFEE

I was in a large furniture warehouse crossed with an airport. Bob Dylan was enraged because he believed I had stolen some of his luggage, his ideas, and a tin of *Maxwell House International French Vanilla* powdered coffee...

I snuck through a number of security gates, and escaped.

storm cloud ... or turd?

I am homeless, all things on my back, the sleeping bag, the jackets, the needles and threads, the bottles and spoons and scarves. I travel and converge with a caravan. They are unmoored balladeers and tinkers, sleeves of tattoos that resemble hogweed. We are welcomed from the dust-blanched alleys, the trees, camp in a woman's living room.

Her house is long, ceilings low; only the maroon paint on the walls and a few mismatched woolen pillows keep it from feeling oppressive, a place where the American soul longs to die while recording every sensation of this most unique death.

Some of our band sacrifices a pig, but we believe the pig *wanted* to go, belly sliced, warm guts tumbling into a pot where voices sing over a perfume made of sulfur and metal and all bruise-colored things—the emotions, the memories, the shit impacted like coal until a diamond is born. The young Bob Dylan with a mustache like a complaint and a hat like a thimble joins the melody over the steaming pot of pig.

This song is to combat a ghost in the house who lurks in all corners. What they don't realize is that their songs have set it free, and it is far more dangerous this way.

Long ago, a body bound the ghost to this house, where it would be condensed in these rooms with too few windows and the stench of long-gone dog. Now it can soar over neighborhoods; gobble families wholesale; leap into swamp water on a lark and possess the gonads of grandfathers who collect too many model airplanes.

The band is glib, goes on tour while I linger in the house inspecting the attic room where the ghost had been bound. It even was left *ghost pellets* to eat, no more than a pet.

I wonder if I should warn the ones who live in its path, the suburban frails, but instead I try to hitch a ride with two sound guys who are recording Afterthought Bob and the No-Good Salutations on tour. They won't stop 'til they get to Wembley.

They shrug at me and say I smell and I disappear into another alley to inspect my underwear which I have worn for many weeks, and is covered with pink and lilac stains, fluids that have come out of me; lemon and mustard, like a field of desert flowers.

"Snobs," I think, and know that as in all dreams, my pith is destined for the road.

ON THE ROAD

I am in a hip European Mod Bar run by children.
One of the beverages is a "hot water in a cold glass."

We were driving through a Nevada-dry vista, through a genuine *ghost town* where the signs on single-story buildings showed advertisements from the seventies, the eighties, but no later. The town had been abandoned for some time. We wondered why—why the entire *town?* Why had people even bothered to settle here, and how did they thrive for several years before calling it quits? Were they forced to leave? There was no water. There were no trees. Only a mile-long patch of buildings on either side of the road punctuated a concourse of endless sand.

We continued on the road until the abandoned town tapered into nothingness and the outline of a vast stadium rose on the horizon.

We parked. We gained passage. Inside the stadium there was a flurry of activity. Oz-like figures scuttled, and teenagers rushed to and from classes. En masse, great quantities of people were preparing for an event to take place, living entire lives within the confines of this stadium.

I was guilty of starting the song, the hum, the sound that would summon the creatures from the deep. I started humming, and perhaps it was with the curiosity of the scab-picker, the scratching of the forbidden itch—but I kept humming, and the ground started shifting. Several people were joining me in this hum, until we could sense, in response to this musical note, that the ground was definitely quaking and something was about to burst from the astroturf.

The synthetic greens severed, and an enormous tentacle burst from the deep and rose above our heads. It was thicker than several men and rose several stories high, and one could only assume that it was attached to a body that would stand higher than the roof of the stadium. We began to run, and on all sides, more tentacles were bursting out of the ground. Whatever process had been started was disrupting all matter.

I saw a boil spontaneously grow and burst on my chest right above the cleavage of a skimpy top. I was wondering who I would bond with in this panic. I was wondering what I could do to stop the tentacles from bursting all over the Earth.

I knew there was one thing, and it had to be done. A certain type of explosive charge could shock them into submission. Their systems were very sensitive to this sort of vibration.

I was running and holding boxes of notebooks, ancient possessions, the only things I would save while on the run. Why had I saved these notebooks? These were probably not the *right* notebooks! Who even knows what to grab in an emergency? None of us really know! We rarely conceive of *real* emergency or exodus in our modern lives. Surely, someone will save us!

As the big tentacles came above ground, other, *smaller* members of the buried civilization were also emerging, bipedal, human-size, resembling humans with black, crenelated frog heads. They were putting on snazzy suits, fedoras...they had a sharp fashion sense, very *Sinatra,* and they started inhabiting the abandoned rooms of the ghost town, especially the newsroom of a local paper, where they resumed their activity using intercoms, tapping away at typewriters, checking the latest *AP* reports, and a myriad of other activities, as if they had merely been gone on a *lunch break,* rather than having hibernated for who knows how many decades. I was really starting to *like* these underground frog-headed ace reporters...they had a *panache,* a sense of get up and go that my fellow humans so often seem to lack...when suddenly the humans figured out the right blast frequency to shock our underground visitors into submission.

There were many loud explosions, and I was left holding a cardboard box of the wrong notebooks on the front lawn of my childhood home, wondering what could have been.

Man, there were parts of my dream right out of a Grimm's fairy tale, or the psychic grist or juice of something *darker,* and Norwegian...

Imagine sunset in a mountain village, a time before the industrial age. Two children, perhaps brother and sister, are sitting in the last long rays of the sun. This golden light illuminates the tall grasses and wildflowers that surround them and it appears that the grass, the flowers, the children's hair and fingers are made of filaments of glass. In this rare sluice of time, the girl finds a gemstone in the grass, as bright as a diamond, as compelling as an opal. It slips out of her hands, almost as if it is hopping out, and is lost.

The children return home and tell their parents about the stone. The next day the father is walking the mountain path, and based on his children's descriptions, he recognizes the spot at the edge of a cliff where his young were sitting, with a balcony view of all the lands below.

He confidently strides over to the spot, but the grass is slippery with dew. He loses his footing and falls from the cliff to his death.

Shortly after this, the girl is diagnosed with a disease that ravages her nerves and leaves her bed-ridden.

She is blonde, with a head shaped like a peanut, and on clean sheets she senses the sun set for another day in the *outer* world she will never run and play in again.

Is there a moral to this story other than that the love of beauty, the *desire to hold pretty stones* can lead to death?

I was in Syracuse, a five-minute walk from the house I grew up in and a street was blocked off with police cars and news cameras because a pride of tame tigers were lounging on the grass of a punk rock troll.

He was a troll, a pipsqueak, the kind of guy who's fifty but still acts fifteen, the kind of guy whose capillaries beat with cartoon blood, as black as Roy Orbison's hair dye, and he believes that treating women like girls with runny noses and no brains will wear them down, down into a kind of slavish devotion.

I was transfixed by his yard of tigers. I overheard a newscaster say they migrated here, and they were mutated, strange; incredibly docile, willing to eat sugary cereal and cheddar cheese from a human palm.

I was hypnotised by their stripes. I walked around them where they lay, and sat on the punk man's porch. He squatted beside me.

"I know who you are," he sneered and kept from looking me in the eye. "You're that writer-chick who has a crush on Bukowski."

This was his gamble: I was supposed to feel that he was *above* me, *onto* me.

"I've never wanted to have sex with Bukowski. And anyway, he's dead," I said, looking at the tigers as the light grew dim.

I was at a punk show and a woman in her early twenties got off stage. The crowd *loved* her. She ranted that no one understood her. I said she was a diva like Liz Taylor, and she called me a diva for presuming I knew what she was made of.

People rushed past me, yelling that we were all mutants and we would die poor, die angry, die with the last lonely dry heave of Planet Earth. But instead of trying to memorize the detail of the dying things, every smile and spider and light bulb and train trestle and leaf, the people stayed in this basement drinking liquids that would make them kiss and then put them to sleep.

I wanted to be one of them, and maybe I did have sex with Bukowski, one of an entire race of Bukowskis. I fell into it so quickly that I was in my grave and the sky was a thousand light years changed before I spoke a truth to a maggot on my tongue:

I was hypnotised by their stripes.

KING VOODOO CRAB:

There he was: King Voodoo Crab; he reclined in his lair like an Egyptian god, and his life was rife with rituals. He wasn't your normal crab. His skin was made of felt like a *Muppet* and his neck was long like a swan and he walked on two legs like a human being, ever-so-graceful. He was fond of wearing suits with ornamental items: top hats, monocles, pocket watches on bejeweled fobs.

He had many lovers. Like King Solomon, his decisions carried the power to spare life and wield death. The town respired with the rhythms of his waking and his sleeping, subjects ruled with a touch of feudalism, soothed by sublime parades in drag.

One of the greatest festivals was coming up, but on its eve, King Crab's doppelgänger appeared.

This was not unusual. King Crab died and was reborn many times. His doppelgängers were instrumental in this process.

They were physical yet ghostly, and it was the job of these shadow selves to lurk, to wait for the right moment to kill him.

After a night of incubation, he would be reborn. His body would lie in state, holy ones and fans praying and susurrating, and in the morning, his dead shell would come back to life.

Every time King Crab came back to life, his body would contain a different version of his soul. When this happened, the doppelgänger would disappear, seemingly into the ether, having served his purpose.

Well this doppelgänger was greedy and killed King Crab too early.

King Crab lay in state with his suit and feathers around his neck, and he looked so beautiful like a rock god in a magazine.

The hours slowly tolled 'til dawn and at the moment his body was supposed to revive, it *didn't*.

The doppelgänger sat uneasy, realizing he would have to fill King Crab's shoes, rather than flitting back to the ether.

The loss of the king was profound. This version of his soul was well-loved. His merriment was legendary.

His harem paced and dug their fingernails in small felt hands to hold back the wails.

The doppelgänger was not so wise, not nearly as merry. He had started out on the *wrong claw* and was stuck having to imitate a greater crab.

EVERY LAST CRUMB:

The man was a world-acclaimed scientist, an elegant polymath. He traveled along with his friends to an abandoned hotel, a high-rise built in the 70's with shag carpets and boxy furniture meant to convert easily into orgy-surfaces.

The hotel had been finished and furnished, but never opened. It was a mystery whether the materials were toxic, or the structure didn't live up to a building inspection, or if, like in a film, the high-rise had been built on an ancient burial ground, sat loaded with spirits ready to strangle a visitor in the night.

There was a caretaker, a woman with hair in the shape of a mushroom. She dressed in boyish clothes. She looked like the famous ice-skater, Dorothy Hamill. She and the scientist fell in love.

He was already thinking of retiring and falling in love gave him the push he needed. When the time came for his friends to leave the hotel and go back to their jobs, he told them he was going to stay.

The scientific community was shocked. This man's innovations were, in some people's minds, the *only* things keeping our species from being defeated by global warming.

Yet he stayed. His hair was already white. He felt more tired and yet more *happy* than he had ever felt in his life.

After he took up residence in the hotel, he stopped writing letters to his friends. At times they would visit him, and he displayed his old sense of humor. He seemed content, though distant in ways they could not define.

Years passed. He *slept*. His wife didn't age. During one visit, his friends noticed that she cooked a special food for him. It looked like a tempeh patty.

In the final night of their stay, the scientist's friends found a way to spill his meal on the floor. They offered him *their* snacks instead, which he accepted with a bashful nonchalance.

Within hours, the scientist was a different man. He openly questioned why he had stayed so long in the hotel. His friends went to sleep *relieved,* convinced that he was finally going to return to the city, to *civilization,* the next day.

Of course, this was not to be.

The *Caretaker* fed him another patty. She turned slowly in the air and rubbed a piece of yarn across his lips. I think it had been dipped in rosemary oil.

She had a power that made the wind blow differently. Insects obeyed her and marched in formation, carrying papers, biting with deadly stings.

The scientist grew sleepy again. His friends escaped the hotel with a great sense of despair.

THE ROBOT EATS PUDDING

I was in a city full of wide, mirrored buildings on a sunny morning. The sky was as blue as the Mediterranean Sea, white hot clouds bouncing back and forth in the mirrored facets of each monolith. I felt *alive*. I was walking in the sun. I was spat out of a hundred diners. I walked on tropical hills in and out of minimarts where my nail polish needs were not met, and no change in my pockets, anyway.

It was then that the robot appeared. It looked like a cybernetic *Joan Rivers* in a motorized scooter, and its purpose in life was to dispense travel advice to pedestrians and serve paper cups of custard from an apparatus concealed under the scarves and folds of its wardrobe. A young Chinese man, barely out of his teens, wracked with a visible internal defect, invited the custard robot up to his hi-rise. She served him in awkward silence, a silence he manifested like a beached whale. After he wiped his mouth, he turned to her and ordered her to do something against her very programming. He forced her to serve herself a cup of custard.

Robots are not meant to eat custard, at least this one wasn't.

She ingested the cold sluice of sugar through her dry rosebud lips. At this point the robot ceased to look like Joan Rivers. She was a mirror image of the man. She had the face, the hands, the wide-eyed stare of the sadist condo-dweller. The robot was so small, so frail, it looked down at its cybernetic foot, wondering if the sadist was going to stomp on it.

After long and sun-filled volumes of silence, the robot escaped on its miniature wheels, more diminutive than ever, to the mirror-shard morn.

At the party, the dead girl is not dead. Her blonde hair is carefully coiffed, has silver highlights, is flat-ironed and sprayed with corkscrew curls at the tips, yet it smells like an ashtray, has spilled food in it, is partially tucked under a wool beret. She wants cocaine and the only reason she's stayed at the party this long is to figure out if anyone has it.

We're in L.A. and the people here *feel* like L.A.— guys with workout bodies who like all the right bands and insist on using the word "hipster" to describe themselves.

Everyone has tattoos and works in "the business." Some fetch coffee for talk show hosts, and others are makeup artists and stylists. I can tell that the dead girl and I are looked at as outsiders.

I ask her the dead girl how the cocaine in L.A. is and she looks at me in surprise, says she doesn't think of me as someone who has taken drugs. She quizzes me, asks me when I've had coke.

She goes on to say coke isn't coke anymore, and I wouldn't now it unless I had it long ago—and I say "2007 to 2009"—and she says nothing to this except she's sick of the party, all these douche-bros and women with smiles as limp as cold turds. She says this loud enough for the room to hear her and saunters out.

I follow her, happy to leave.

Once we get outside, she doesn't leave, though. We go out the back door, fragrant plumeria night, yet she lingers in the yard and stumbles up to the front door, looking in the window, seeing if there is anyone new she hasn't seen, anyone new to figure out, get something from.

She may be dead, but she's got money and she's ready to buy anything.

The people inside see us peeking through the door and open it and let us back in.

We sit on a sofa near a bed which is inexplicably in

the living room.

A gorgeous man covered from head to toe in silver glitter and wearing designer shoes with a horn-shaped heel enters. He has whiskers. He is a silver cat.

He flops down on the bed and starts talking with the other guests, and I think to myself, *finally someone interesting!* But he begins to gossip and roll on the bed with the others and I lose interest.

There is a warrant for my arrest and I am riding my bike on a highway past red and orange leaves. I go from town to town on highways and over bridges and meet drifters when I'm squatting to piss.

Finally I make it to a cafe, where I change from my traveling man's clothes and put on the Laurie Anderson head and crimson leather jacket to enter the cafe where all of the tables are aluminum, and Christmas music is playing.

I wonder if I'll ever get home, or what that means anymore.

I was a surgeon operating on a woman's face on a city street at 3 AM, the night summery, fragrant, the soil black and full of worms, my scalpel-strokes lit by the wattage of a high-powered lamp, the kind electric companies use for late-night repairs.

I removed several slices of a red bell pepper and two unripe tomatoes from the hollow beneath her eye, and sewed her up again. It didn't occur to me that she might need these vegetables later. Perhaps her face could not run through its daily functions without the presence of subcutaneous vegetables.

As the dawn neared, a witch led me to a churchyard and sang a song, and it hardly mattered what the song was about, so I say. It was a eulogy, a reunion song, a promise of a new beginning, but dreams lie.

Once upon a time she looked in her mirror and saw my face. Once upon a time we drilled holes in each other's brains. Her voice was high and reminded me of feathers dyed an artificial blue, blue the color of Windex and carnations at a junior prom.

We move on. We compete with phantoms.

VAMPIRE LOVER AND THE UNHOLY PIRANHAS:

I was renting a house in a small town, a house with wooden panels and very high ceilings, and spots that smelled like mold and death, but I told myself a good coat of paint would keep out the mold and death for at least ten years, and over the course of several weeks it was claimed as a clubhouse for kids into fantasy and horror and unclassifiable forms of psychological calculus.

The house grew to have many floors and homeless teens and gamer nerds and young men who hadn't changed their clothing in two years who would count pebbles in a personal mania and have heated discussions even in the midst of snoring.

The woods grew thicker around the house and I heard that vampires were near. One was a woman with a spider-thin body and short brown hair and wild brown eyes and we were magnetically attracted to each other. I knew that she wanted to bite me, and that the bite would *kill* rather than turning me into one of the undead.

I had the argument in my head that we could have a wild woodland romance, that she had real feelings for me which I could detect on her many returns to the perimeter of the house, when I struggled to push her out the front door. I told myself that we *needed* to see each other, we had become a part of each other.

For a time she disappeared. I interrogated a young redhaired woman who was camped out in the house about a "witch" she saw, hoping to get answers, but her witch had blue eyes and seemed arthritic. Not *my* vampire.

The young woman was traumatized after telling me of her witch, which was not my witch. I felt an obligation to soothe her.

We walked along a beach. We walked through the night, and into the dawn. We saw a battalion of kayak people preparing to do arabesques in the water.

When I approached the surf, an eyeless fish in the

shape of a triangle started biting and killing the kayak people.

Eyeless fish surrounded us. I trapped one in a plastic bag. It escaped and followed us. They were able to move on land.

One could never escape the feeling that one was going to be bitten to death by potential lovers or hacked-up reanimated meat in this dream, but let me tell you, the *sunrise* was beautiful.

MY FATHER AND THE DEALER AND BRIAN JONES

I was young and poor in an enormous city and going up and down the stairs of a run-down apartment building where everyone was painting their rooms at the same time, and I abruptly ran into my father.

Let me catch you up on things: He didn't raise me. We have only met twice. We have not had a conversation—as much as we could have, he in broken English, I in broken French—for twenty-five years.

In this dream, however, messages went back and forth. I took a plane to Paris, to the small Left Bank apartment where he lived, his walls lined with Ravi Shankar records, the Ashanti fetish masks which he compulsively collected, and dented overly heavy mahogany dressers inherited from his mother. We were trying to get re-acquainted.

My father was dating a mysterious woman who looked like Eartha Kitt. All three of us were in a fine dining establishment in the 60's. In this world, the 1960's never ended. If you stick around long enough, you'll even meet *Brian Jones*.

Marijuana was legal in all dining establishments, yet my father was embarrassed by what was happening: He moved the candle away from the spot on the table where his girlfriend was rolling a joint with an expert precision—perhaps *too* expertly. She was crushing special potions and taking gel-like fluids out of vials, and mixing all of these ingredients into the innocent green leaves, mashing them like the contents of a mojito. She had a sleek plastic case with a built-in mashing tray that looked so tidy, so lethal, for these occasions.

This was a special cigarette and it would give a special high and both my father and I had the feeling that his girlfriend's private income came from assembling these.

The more I smiled and asked to try the joint, the more stern the woman's expression became. I was at first eager to have it, but the longer she mashed and added to it, the more sinister it became, and I thought of feigning

87

a stomach-ache or some discreet reason I had to leave the table so that I wouldn't have to blow my brains out permanently with this sacred spliff.

The restaurant was on the top floor of a hotel. I managed to leave the table, then the restaurant.

I wandered the halls, and I found myself entering a deluxe suite upholstered floor to celing in intricate paisley fabrics. Cameramen swarmed around the room where a ritual was taking place, a ritual staged specifically for a film.

My eyes were on the hair, the legs, the *boots*. Verushcka was prancing slowly, dramatically in a circle. The light came in chalky from the windows, so it was hard for me to tell if her lean over-the-knee boots were black or a very royal dark purple. Her long blonde hair and the loincloth she had on were swaying, *swaaaaaaying* with each slow-motion step she took around the doctors. The doctors—in lab coats, surgical scrubs, the whole theatrical nine yards—were filling up syringes near the buckets that held several bottles of champagne. The buckets and the syringes were in the center of the room, piled up like the offerings on an altar.

Brian Jones swallowed a glass of champagne and asked to go first. I was standing right next to him. His hair was very thick, very clean. He seemed pretty together at first—dashing, coherent, not the drooling mess you see in most of the historic photographs.

Then he got his injection. Within thirty seconds he ducked his head under the paisley altar he was leaning on and vomited into a champagne bucket. When he wiped his mouth and raised his head from the shadows, his eyes were glassy and he gave a simpleton's grin.

"I'm SOOOOOO druuuuuunk," he said. Even though whatever was happening to him was caused by the injection, it struck me as funny that he'd say he was drunk.

By this time I *was* Veruschka and I was next to get the shot. I didn't want it. There was something sinister about *this* room, too. There was something sinister, fake, about the idea of a ritual, of anything sacred happening here. Who were these priestly doctors, and why did all the brilliant people being shot-up have to be total messes incapable of tying their *shoes* afterwards? Was any of this *worth* it?

I started to scheme how to get out of this room without causing a panic. I would pretend I was going to have a costume change so I would be wearing something special for my "injection scene." Then I would escape...

IT'S NATURAL

Marianne Faithfull falls down a flight of stairs, which paralyzes the nerves in her face. She calls it "Natural Botox."

WAXY CLOWN

The girl is an obsessive case. She sits in the living room of a rental house attempting to reproduce a legendary missing Warhol painting in which a child with blue hair is on a swingset, bits of copper wire attached to the canvas, and a cheap vintage brooch is the sun.

It is San Francisco and I ride with two witches, and it is the future. One of the witches is Snow White and the other is Snow Black. The people of the future can no longer afford shoes and wander through the display areas barefoot or in mismatched socks. Snow White and Snow Black look at things I can't afford and I am suddenly on the phone with my dead grandmother.

She is asking me how I am enjoying France. I am in San Francisco and pretend I am in France but realize she is walking toward me holding the phone in her hand and will realize the folly of my fine and beautiful prevarications.

They are *Ancient Aussie Aliens,* I am told. They meet with Native Americans, a sacred convergence in the desert, but isn't everything desert already? This film is a rehearsal so that you will recognize the process of leaving your body when it happens: The camera pans slowly across the faces of the aliens and humans gathered and the voiceover tells us that *primitive is relative, after all.*

In aisles that rise to the ceiling, the aliens and the primitives are represented by cheap driftwood memorabilia sold at top dollar prices. I handle an elaborate flute, and semi-digested dreamcatchers, and earmuffs, and holographic shoes, and want to devour everything, take every item inside of my body and grow thinner rather than fatter with their weight.

The sun is shining and we are at the edge of the city. The sound of waves lapping against the shore is discarded like a cheap white noise machine. The man in a canary yellow Chevy picks us up. It has no markings of a taxi, yet it feels as if he is providing a service, and payment will be exacted one way or another.

He is wearing a mask over his face that looks like melted plastic and wax. It barely conceals his features, and strands of a wig cover his pate, through which tufts of his natural hair are barely visible. From the flaps of skin at the back of his neck, I can tell he is older. It is a clown mask. He wears a pierrot jumpsuit, his hands affixed to the steering wheel with a mechanical concentration.

He drives us into the countryside. At first the witches are with me, but I realize as the ride progresses that I am alone with this clown. I sense that he has killed many people, however the thought has not yet registered in his head that he should kill me.

He drives in silence. Since I entered the car, he has not spoken a word. He takes me to the country, the terrain hilly and green, orchards to either side of the road. The more I stare at the mask on his face, it appears to fuse with the flesh of his neck as if there is no line of demarcation.

He pulls into a parking lot in front of an apartment building, burnished wooden beams, an 80's *aesthetique* where one would expect a farmhouse to be. A sign in front of the building advertises $308 monthly rent for a one-bedroom, and I run through a mental experiment of what it would be like to live here, so isolated, surrounded by apple orchards and morning mist, and not another artist or existentially depressed writer for fifty square miles around.

I watch the clown take his keys out of the ignition. In an even voice I ask him if he wants me to follow him upstairs, and he nods YES.

I follow him up the external stairway to a balcony where a party is taking place. We enter the apartment and it is full of old ladies, knitted afghans, *Hummels* and other ceramic knickknacks, birthday cards, ten-year old "US" magazines, and the clutter you would expect to find in such a place.

It feels like a family reunion is taking place. Younger relatives of the old ladies are visiting, nervous boys in soccer jerseys and young couples who cannot wait to escape. These visitors eye me with distrust, but the old ladies embrace me, offering me food, an array of cooked blonde brownies and salsas and chicken wings that appear to be flavored with dehydrated lemon-garlic powder.

Despite how friendly the ladies are, I don't trust their food, and gingerly pluck three blueberries from a colander as my only snack.

I nod to the clown that I am leaving. We both go out the door, tethered to each other for an indefinite and possibly eternal *odyssey* through time.

THE INJECTABLE MAN

I was buying a house in a rural zone, and I took a long bus ride to get to it.

I was dropped off on a dirt road and went inside. One of my friends was curious about the house and showed up with her teenaged daughter, who ran over to a poster of the cast of the Rocky Horror Picture Show that was on the wall. The girl violently tore it off the wall and ripped it into little pieces.

I had given up on the house idea and was helping "The Injectable Man." He was very small. He was shrinking by the hour. When I first met him he was as small as a fingernail, wearing a scuba suit. Soon he was microscopic and hitching a ride on my hand across a busy entrance to a subway station. Every brass rail I touched, I hoped he hadn't fallen off.

His goal was to shrink to a subatomic size where an alien dive bar was.

When small enough to fit on the bar stools, he could drink for an eternity. The bar was inside a woman's body.

THE DYING CHILD

His father is a star, singing along to a prerecorded version of himself. The child is hooked up to pulleys and suction devices, and as the hours pass he looks increasingly like a turtle, purple and distorted.

Mother is Doris Day. This is a telethon. An athlete with muscles like steaks, like stripper poles, solid and oiled; it was a minor injury, a concussion, so why is he dead now? Why did machines come to eclipse the rhythms of his autonomic function, his corn color-hair, body turned to cheese curl?

Star Wars is coming. Our heroes are young again and fifty feet long.

A party after the auditions in a Victorian-era house, summer night, abandoned mine shafts three blocks away: I was allowed to enter with a flashlight and the walls danced around me, geode-ragged, complete, tongue-colored.

These walls don't need mortal input. All over again my destiny, the earth a womb rather than a watery grave.

A CORONER AND AN AIRPLANE PILOT, TO MAKE ENDS MEET.

I was wandering around a city and the weather was predicted to be in the 120s for several weeks in a row. Speculations filled the media that everything—the oceans, food supplies, animals and the weather would be off-kilter permanently after this. Yeah, global warming, but that's old news. An asteroid was on course to graze the earth's stratosphere so closely that a lot of people were thinking in terms of their last embrace:

Which *restaurant* do you want to be in when it hits? And with *whom?* Would you prefer to be driving in your car? In a doctor's office? On a *beach?* In a bunker, with liquidation-sale Pringles, a footbath of potable water, paper porn for when the electrical grid goes down, Memory Foam slippers and a wall of Quaker Oats? Do you run into the woods with a picture of your wife, or the woman you wish you had been with instead?

All my life I've laughed at suicide parlors as a corny device in a Charlton Heston movie, especially when the only character I liked in the flick decides to use one, but in a sudden emotional seizure it makes sense to me that people would *turn off,* be incinerated, rather than form a choir in the steaming post-disaster chaos.

The coroner is in his house with another coroner. They are best friends. For some reason it is hard for them to attract and keep other friends. They look like overgrown metalheads, or gamers. One is stocky with a balding pate and Pan-like features. The other is extraordinarily tall, a human chopstick, his head crowned with frizzy blond hair in a ponytail. This blond one is also an airplane pilot, and he is leaning on the railing of a stairway in this nicely-appointed house, laughing and comparing notes.

They brought a body to the house. The asteroid hasn't hit yet, but the streets are on fire. The people **OUT** there are strange. Our odd couple are stuck with a body that needs to be embalmed, and they've taken it home.

It is the body of a very important person. It is naked.

I stand over the body and my eyes are caressing its shapes, rather than my hands. I don't recognize whose body it is, only that it is important and needs to be preserved so that people after the disaster have a memory of who this *was,* and why the mind the body once housed was important.

The house is large. I begin to roam its corridors. There is a hallway to the left of the living room and a teenaged girl is inside. She is seventeen, and very shy. She is shy…and she is angry.

She is an artist. She sculpts vaginas. They are less than a foot tall and made of clay. Some are carved from wood and stand upright; pure and elemental shapes. When I walk into her room, I realize that I am her mother.

Her lanky hair and blank eyes let me know that I am not getting past her screen.

I ask to look at her sculptures, and she moves one across a table for me to see, but I realize that she does not know me, or need to know me, and she does not expect me to help her in any way when the disaster hits.

I leave the room for a moment and when I reach the living room, it is dark. The lights are off, and while it is still afternoon, the sky has taken on a greenish cast, as if there is an eclipse.

I find myself crying—*crying actual tears!*—something I rarely do. I am crying that everything has come to this; even if the asteroid is natural, even if our species' greed-wish which amounts to a death-wish is natural. Even if my typing this, and you reading it on a page is natural.

What have we let ourselves become? And when will we ever find the energy to overthrow the worst in us to start again?

No, there is no improving with **AGAIN.** The same thing happens every time. So the question should be, when will we overthrow the worst in us to keep things from getting *even worse?*

There is no asteroid in sight.

A man made of harelips, catheter tips, and overdraft fees walks into a bar. It is New Year's Eve and the one shaped like a cigarette sits with the beefcake contagion, the poet on the rise. I am in a banquet hall and drunk housewives in cleavage-revealing sheaths are on the prowl in every direction I look. I try to find a place where the three of us—the cigarette, the visiting dignitary, and the vagina dentata—can sit.

I end up standing on a table singing a Broadway showtune about a man I dare to shoot an arrow at me. He holds the arrow in the quiver and I start, while singing, to sway my body in such a way that my hand will catch the arrow. The arrow goes through my hand and I pull it out, but I don't bleed or feel the pain.

The stroke of midnight comes, but it looks like the stroke of noon; a milky light leers through every window and makes me feel that we are hovering in an indeterminate sluice of time that is only *cosmetically* labeled with clothing and the names of dictators...yet as insubstantial as it is, this time encompasses my growth from puberty to our current age when my skin starts changing to orange rind and all of the animals are dying. Can you believe I hear this pronouncement?

"In a way, it's good that the human race is killing all of these animals."

"What animals?" I ask.

A rave cloak sways at his feet. His head is as wide as a pumpkin.

"You know, all of the species going extinct."

"Why on earth would you say that?"

"Because they are making room for the ones that will evolve in the gaps."

I speak in a voice of mirth and dismay, a complicated move:

"Instead of God in the gaps, you mean *evolution* in

the gaps..."

The empty spaces, like frozen tundra, where birdsong will be gone and forests will catch on fire with renewed vigor, and the elderly male lemur will wander around for five years wondering where his mate is except there are no more mates...only the last of this line, the last of that line...making way for...*more evolution!* This is not a new idea.

I take a final look at the man who believes we are making way for more evolution. His breath smells like a sewer.

"You really *are* a glass half-full kind of guy!"

The emissary with tat-sleeves says I look good when I smile but I wonder why I was waiting for this pronouncement. Does every tattoo on his body see my smile?

My words are not always knives. I bleed and coo, despite the photographic evidence of eternity.

THE ITALIAN MINI-MOGUL OF CHEESE

I was part of a traveling "holiday cheer" caravan that would go to small towns and seduce wealthy supermarket managers into adding our holiday-themed decorations to each superstore.

In one small town there was this middle-aged Italian mini-mogul who *LOVED CHEESE*. He was buff, he worked out, he wore the finest suits and tried to maintain his sybaritic tastes while camped out in this backwater cornfield. When our caravan arrived, I convinced him to let me add subliminal cheese decorations to every inch of the store—little reminders to eat cheese near the ceilings, and the rubber curbs by the floor—near the bathrooms, and the magazine racks. *CHEEEEEESE,* everywhere. I told him confidentially: "You and I might think about cheese every hour, we have good taste. *They* don't, yet."

He instantly fell in love with me and offered me a lacy piece of something Swiss. I had to spit out the cheese already in my mouth to get to the new cheese.

This supermarket mogul, he also felt, as he saw his graying temples in the mirror, that he was getting *out of touch* with the proletariat culture, so he, with a wild hair up his ass, did this: He stayed up all night drinking and mopping the floors in his superstore, and at 4 AM when the kitchen help came in, a tall Lincoln-like supervisor gave the mogul a scolding:

"Sir, we really appreciate you being our boss and all, but we prefer to do these jobs ourselves..."

After leaving the store, drunk and feeling accomplished, the gray-templed Italian mini-mogul strutted through summertime parking lots—*ahhh,* Americana.

He was intent on visiting the caravan, and me. He was smitten with his *compatriot in cheese.* In this part of the dream, I was a 1940's floozie with twenty boyfriends and a toddler and cut-off shorts, and I had just had an abortion earlier in the day, so I wasn't feeling like whooping it up, but...I saw the mogul's twinkling eyes and gray temples at the door before the dawn came around and felt the **LIFE** under him, and I knew that, like anyone in a traveling caravan, we choose **LIFE**, we choose motion, we stay up all night, because there might not be a tomorrow...

The world, it has reverted, grown visibly wild. City blocks are broken open with trees and vines and wildflowers, and it is not a good idea to be alone, ever.

Cars still work, if you are lucky enough to be able to repair one and find fuel for it on a black market with diminishing supplies. Many people live in compounds, but some couples still go it alone in suburban houses, only to be found later hung and shot by nomads, their stockpiles looted, the upholstery of their reading chairs and their stacks of decorating magazines left behind as odes to a long run of human civilization now shuttered, kaput.

In this reality, one is forced to be a nomad. Don't let anyone catch your scent!

I am traveling with two others, nomads like myself, and we stay in any "clean" house for three days at the longest.

Young people have acclimatized to the stability of constant strife, but groups of senior citizens sit proudly on their mowed lawns, in patches of early-afternoon sun, swaying in rocking chairs, wearing carefully-buttoned cardigans, reading long-expired copies of the Saturday Evening Post as if they are doing their best, nearly a century after they were created, to impersonate Norman Rockwell paintings.

These proud enclaves of seniors are mowed down eventually, but it is the flavor of the thing, defiance of lawlessness, that gives them continued meaning.

We loot old shopping malls and machine shops and elementary schools. We loot barns and wine cellars and parts of the suburbs that have been walled-off as communes.

We travel as three, but leave our third party, an old man in overalls with gentle Henry Fonda eyes, eyes like a Charlie Brown squiggle, like coffee beans, on the side of a dirt road, where he will most likely be killed for sport within an hour.

Why do we leave him there? His eyes are pleading with us to keep him in the car with us, safe, in motion, but his eyes are also resigned. There is a fate in this reality that one cannot put off indefinitely.

We break into an institution which was once posh, with wall-to-wall carpeting and discreetly inlaid lighting fixtures, one of a series of monoliths in a high-tech industrial park.

We are watching a music video of a man who is now middle-aged.

In the video, he is in his very early twenties, angry blue eyes, jet black hair, girded loosely in a leather bondage cap and chaps. He is singing about how much he needs to be tied up, how much he needs a spanking. The expression on his youthful face tells us that nothing in this world could really excite him except the annihilation of all life.

He and a series of leather-chaps copycats get into machines that resemble Iron Maidens, where their rear ends are exposed, and they are spanked so hard that they radiate a pain that is harnessed through sensors of the machines and into a NORAD-style missile system.

Nuclear missiles, which the singer calls "bullshit cum" are ejaculated all over the planet after a sufficient group spanking—the slowing arcs of each missile's progress shown on glowing screens above the masochists' heads.

The pop star is middle-aged now, and much has happened since he recorded that video. He is even more jaded, and the skin of his face, like the skin of many older British men, has grown rubbery, like overchewed gum stretched across his ample jaw.

He is about to be interviewed, about to give commentary on the course of his life, our life. He gives off the air of an old-fashioned gangster. He is capable, but could be killed quickly.

CHRYSALIS FACE

I once dated a sadist and now he carries a shovel, a skip in his stride to beat the old man to a prize.

The sadist, the rich old man, and my body hasten to the corner of a swimming pool which has turned into a bog. Chlorine vapors, sun, a chain-link fence add a sedative quality to our suburban frieze.

We see crystalline blue, the enameled bottom and sides of the pool through ripples of clear water which is with every step obscured by a layer of seaweed, leaves, and growing things.

The mass of fungi, seaweed, and branches rise from the water's surface like a throne, and lying on the throne, as if sleeping, is the body of a child, a boy in a three-piece tweed suit.

How did I arrive at this place, on a globe of supermarkets and clouds? I should a be a slave a thousand times over, and yet I am free enough, and my eyes focus on the child.

His face is so decomposed, and so serene. His face is made of a semi-transparent wax. Light ripples through his cheeks, his nose, a prisoner without will.

There is an urgency among the men that this boy is a rare one, must be claimed, plucked from his throne.

In being overly done, he has just begun. He is the chrysalis-face.

RE-ANIMATED AND THE FOUNTAIN OF AGE:

When people I know are dead (and he has been dead for almost twenty years) appear in my dreams, I am wary of them. There is no way that any *positive* force could so stiffly re-animate these bodies, bodies that don't behave like they did when they were living.

The dead re-animated in my dreams seem to be stuck in mindless loops, whether fixing roofs or washing dishes, without smiles or words, and are only dimly aware of my presence. In this case, the dead man was my grandfather, and the injury on his head was huge and fresh—a cracked skull.

Perhaps most disturbing about the hole in the back of his head, as wide as a monk's shaved tonsure, was that no blood was coming out.

Once awake, I look at the date on my phone and realize that this would have been his 97th birthday.

The dream continues:

The house has been dislodged in time. It is the house I have grown up in with my grandparents. The season appears to be summer. Vines, bushes, and marshy flowers sprout around the house, thriving in the humidity.

This lawn, and the lawns of neighbors, roar with an inner life that at once feels ancient and playfully young. A patch of five trees is a forest. There are fiefdoms of pine needles, rivers of *nepenthe,* grottoes of birch twigs and broken shale. Mourning doves perch above. They sing, despite the fact that flying away would bring them instant death.

You see, if you try to leave the house, you start to age. I am with a friend who is a very vain man. The further we step from the driveway and walk for several blocks, we change.

We are in a city. I look at my reflection in a storefront window. I look like a celebrity who has disappeared for the past thirty years and no one knows anymore what twilight she inhabits, whether she is living or dead. I look like *Loni Anderson.* The skin on my face, neck and chest is puckered, elderly, despite my lipstick remaining as flawless as it was fifteen minutes ago, when we left the house.

I try to explain to my friend that we must not walk any further or our bodies will age so much that we will die where we are standing.

I don't want to alarm him. He doesn't seem entirely aware of how we have aged as I herd him back to the safety of the house and watch the youth return to my hands.

We are trapped.

(Okay, it wasn't a fountain of age....so much as a *sidewalk!*)

He is...the chrysalis face!

NAKED BREAKDOWN SMURF

I dreamed about a six-foot-tall Smurf who had a nervous breakdown along a highway and was found trudging slowly, uncertainly, his fur matted, his eyes hollow, his buttocks lean and exposed to the public like those of an infamous drifter.

It was dark. A number of us, his "friends," were in a car, all dolled up for a night on the town. The car had slowed, and the driver was endeavoring to move at the pace the breakdown Smurf was walking. Some of us were trying to talk to him through an open window, see if he was responsive. I felt dread, dread for the black hole inside this matted naked Smurf. I knew this would not end well.

What is the human race? A bunch of seething beasts constantly feeling wronged, racing toward the next and temporary salvation, no better than a planet populated by naked breakdown Smurfs. Our perfumes and the fineness of our silk; our mastery over fast cars, and the accolades we get may temporarily relieve us of the black holes forever creeping up from our mitochondria, creeping up in the rhythms of our hearts, creeping up from the calloused pads of our feet and our earliest memories of the crib to consume us.

Is madness like a hit song? Is death inevitable? *Yes*.

See what this Smurf dream brings *out* of me? You'd better hope I don't dream of smack-addicted My Little Ponies or *Schizoid-Break Miss Piggy* tomorrow night.

I drink White Russians and listen to the Stooges at the *1201 Club* until the bar turns into a house party. The ceiling is made of crow feathers. The feathers are singed where spotlights sit in their mounts and dare us to grow old. He was once a coke dealer, grew lean and traveled with supermodels, a bottle blonde-heiress, however at this point his body has learned to dilate the cervix of time.

We sneak to the freezer where he keeps balloons of heroin and I have hidden individually-wrapped homemade caramels. We keep running into each other as we grab our addictions from the freezer, puzzle pieces hidden behind racks of frozen spinach, tuneless microwave tostadas.

"You're just like me," he says, knowing that I can't stop grabbing the brittle caramel blobs and he cannot stop taking what he needs until we are certain the icy berth yields no more.

I watch stagger-drunk Marilyn lurch across the living room and know that in her head the entire universe is made of her respiration, a pulsation of blood in her fingers; we are converted to pure concept...*has-beens, competition, salvation*...when her necklace breaks.

A man masturbates on my stomach after a waiter brings a steaming bowl of Indian daal. The waiter has wires on his undercarriage, maybe metal joists.

ACCOMPANIED BY SARGOSSIAN:

The residents of the apartment building were being priced out, packing up the elaborately-assembled textiles, woods, tusks, and marbles of their salons and bedchambers; kitchens retrofitted with beakers and pipettes that lent the gleam of laboratories. Over time these residents had accumulated the totems of wealth, yet they could no longer afford Manhattan.

(a century ago this was a warehouse lit by gas-lamps, ceilings high, storage crates stacked like coffins, the scents of dung and grain and ale mashed into wooden floorboards; no more—)

The vast room was empty but for a sofa. On it sat the famous man. Some saw him as a literary sage, a once-in-a-generation thinker whose scope bridged the interpersonal and the political with poetry that read like a prayer.

He was tall, even when seated, white temples in a shock of black hair coiffed with the detail of a wedding cake. He wore a button-down shirt made of a casually expensive linen and jeans in a style that made me think of the year nineteen-eighty-two.

I was approaching him with a book I had found by the window, a poetry anthology. I did not know he was a famous writer yet—I only considered him as one of the many people moving out.

I handed him the book, open to a certain page. He asked me what I thought of a poem on the page and I said I didn't engage with it, and he dismissed me.

I picked up the book again, found another poem, and handed it to him.

He peered into it deeply, nodding as if to express that I had finally chosen one which was good, surprisingly good. He peered into the lines, as if seeking something beyond the lines; they jolted him.

After he left the room a person handed me a book which he had written to illuminate me on how important the man was. His last name was Sargossian.

The grim, mushroom-colored light leaking through the windows was dimming to night. The longer I looked out the window, the higher the building became.

I sensed that a disaster was about to happen and that I shouldn't be in this room, high off the ground, when it did. I went down the hall in search of an elevator. When I found one, Sargossian was standing at its doors.

I pressed the button to go down, and it went up.

Sargossian stood by my side as this happened, radiating a silent but smug knowledge of how this reality worked.

When I got out, I was on the same floor. I watched as other residents pressed the button to go down, and the elevator moved, and the arrow glowed UP and we got out exactly where we started.

Something was incubating under the building and it was growing. Plate-glass windows in the halls showed that we were now thirty floors off the ground.

Sargossian knew the building's secrets. He took my arm and showed me a rural road, a small town with a main street built on a singular hill, time passing in a century called the Nineteenth and then the Twentieth, a candy factory blanketing the streets with the oppressive, festive scent of artificial fruit.

And as he waved his arm, the vision passed, and we were in the building again, and it was growing, now forty, now fifty floors tall, and the disaster was about to strike, but I couldn't go down; only up, accompanied by Sargossian.

I learned how to write in constellation. A flashing light was beneath the stars, like an old-fashioned computer cursor, and I was typing a word in the sky using elaborate arm gestures when Neil Young interrupted me for a passionate kiss, which continued to get more erotic, and at one point it felt like his entire hand was slithering inside my mouth.

Men were pretending to be astronauts inside their office cubicles. Women wore black lipstick and elaborate European folk costumes for a ritual about to begin.

You were there, too. You were holding candles and rushing through the rooms of a Catholic school after hours, weaving between rows of empty desks, winter easing closer, waiting for the sun to set.

GLOSSARY

Congratulations! You've made it to Jennifer Robin's *Pop-Cultural Decoder!*

The following entries will hopefully *educate* you, add flesh to the bones of random names and references that have appeared in the preceding pages, or at the very least they will make you realize how very, very old I truly am…

featuring…

Jim Morrison… there once was a man who bound his lower half in leather. Snake who tried to be a bull, but the bull's bride yields a pipe of Now-forgetting. Sideways lightning, noon toll, sodden wings, pillar of ash. Does Jim Morrison or Van Morrison howl louder? Morris-none and neither as much as Beefheart. I recently learned that my mother was living in Paris at the time of his overdose. Found in a tub, or a club called the Rock 'n' Roll Circus, the body moved from its urinal to avoid liability, like a corpse in a murder mystery, wrapped in a cloak or carpet; sunk in the bubbly. Her morning walk took her past his building, and on this day the ramparts were surrounded by mourners and reporters. *Once-Jim,* having long abandoned his leather pants and taken up heroin, planning on making a comeback, *really* proving himself, even though he had already been the Lizard King (who can do anything). But even the Lizard King has amnesia, is subject to *spells* like the rest of us.

Neil Young… who loves Mother Earth, and when my grandfather heard me playing Young's *American Stars 'n Bars* he must have wondered why a teenaged girl in New York was listening to the kind of music he tried to escape when he moved out of Missouri many decades before. But Neil Young isn't really country; I would have said to him if he had asked; he is *cosmic.* He is a shapeshifter. He is my friend, the *Canadian Pan.*

Howard Stern... a man shaped like Ichabod Crane with a mane of black hair and a chicken's grin who made a career out of asking celebrities embarrassing questions on live radio; speculating on which political figures patronize dungeons and have prosthetic breasts. He was called a *shock jock,* but now everyone is a shock jock, even the people who say they are reforming society.

Eartha Kitt... iconoclastic intellect promoted as "sex kitten," born on a cotton plantation in North Carolina, sent to live with her aunt in New York City, the once-famous Mecca of Theatre of which Frank Sinatra once sang, "If I can make it there, I'll make it anywhere." She slept on subways, worked as a teenaged seamstress; her talents of singing and oration earned her scholarships that led to international fame. She discussed phenomenology with Sartre, handed Sidney Poitier a gift-wrapped bat, played Helen of Troy with Orson Welles, performed in seven languages, sang Piaf, interviewed Einstein, dined with Nehru, and was the voice of *Skippy Peanut Butter.* Best friend of James Dean who foresaw his fiery roadside death in a Porsche Spyder. Blacklisted by the Johnson administration after her criticism of the Vietnam War and America's treatment of returning veterans—far more than *Catwoman.* No shopping mall or cafe can go through the month of December without playing the song *Santa Baby* five-thousand times; the Eartha Kitt version, not the Madonna.

Iggy Pop... a primal scream masquerading as a human being. His navel leads to the center of the Earth.

Smurfs... in the land once known as **BELGIUM** a cartoonist invented 99 blue gnomes ruled by a bearded dude named Papa and hunted by a wizard named Gargamel, who wants to boil them in a pot. Why are all 99 Smurfs male? What hypnotic power does Papa hold over them? Gargamel invents an evil *Brunette Female Smurf* to seduce the boys to his pot, but Papa turns her blonde with a special incantation, which makes her obedient, and sigh and shriek when things go bump in the night. I tortured a friend on a 2-hour long road trip by making him play *The Smurfs Party Time* cassette, featuring quite a lot of conspicuously Abba-era Smurf disco songs. I was 28.

Brian Jones... baggy-eyed blonde maestro of *The Rolling Stones* who was responsible for their melodic psychedelic direction and the bruises on *La Pallenberg's* arms; prone to jealous rages in Moroccan villas; a Cheshire Cat crossed with Dickens' Tiny Tim, died of an overdose, or drowning, or at the hand of his gardener.

Mike Nesmith... member of the pre-fab televised pop group *The Monkees;* devastatingly handsome and he knows it; prone to wearing a lumberjack hat and playing the straight man until the success of Gram Parsons, when Nesmith decides he's going to quit the group and launch (an ultimately unsuccessful) musical career as a psychedelic cowboy *too.* Penned the unbelievably lovely song *Tapioca Tundra,* which I would like to have played at my funeral or to accompany whatever it is people will do when I finally expire in the year 2142.

Bob Dylan... the only man who has spent his lifetime trying to escape Bob Dylan. Dresses like a Roma marriage broker in the year 1932, and he really likes horses.

Patsy and Edina, of the British comedy Ab Fab... two Swinging Sixties *muses *groupies *omnivores decide to work in the fashion industry and contend with obsolescence once the 90's *clomp* in; they will do anything to obtain more *Moschino, coke* or *bolly*—played to savage effect by the *immortal* Joanna Lumley and Jennifer Saunders.

James Spader... egg-eyed king of the crows, former hunk, chaotic neutral. In Hollywood dramas often typecast as a lawyer or investment banker with a taste for kink and a *heart of gold.*

Roy Orbison... resembling a waxworks dummy even in the flower of his youth; a man who emanates the quality of excruciating loneliness as an (effective) mating call.

Jim Henson's Muppets... these gemstone-colored frogs and doodlebugs and pigs with diva personalities originated on the children's television series *Sesame Street*. A phenomenon of felt and feathers rather than a *puppet show;* channeling something so pure and exuberant that even when they *did vaudeville,* they did not seem of this Earth. The songs *Moving Right Along* and *Rainbow Connection* can still pry tears out of the waxworks known as *moi*. The Muppets could've saved the Earth but they ended up selling pizza. You had to be there.

Alice Cooper... at the time of this writing he is septuagenarian golf star, but in the late Sixties this preacher's son and his band of Detroit merrymakers delivered some of the most surreal hard rock on the planet, specifically the Zappa-produced album, *Pretties for You*. The group attracted the attention of Salvador Dali and the ire of religious groups, who believed that the highlight of his stage show—pantomiming his own decapitation every night—could usher in the era of the *Antichrist*.

Syd Barrett... Victorian doll whose imagination produced pop songs as kaleidoscopic and obtuse as the masterwork done by the patricidal resident of Bedlam, Richard Dadd: a painting titled *The Fairy Feller's Master Stroke*. Sex symbol at 22, recluse by 30; given too much acid, they say. Godfather of a dozen musical genres: Haunting before *Goth*. Androgynous before *Bowie*. *Weird Folk* before Robyn Hitchcock and Jad Fair. Subject of my twenty-something fantasies.

Laverne and Shirley... a tee-vee show about two young women who work in a brewery and live as roommates in the late Nineteen-Fifties. I compulsively watched them in reruns as a child, with particularly vivid memories of Saturday nights, 7 pee-em in the dead of winter when my mother and grandmother shuffled me to church, and we would return to eat spaghetti with the homemade meatballs I stridently refused to eat because I believed that cows had as much right to live and use their muscles and organ meat as I did. The smell of *Kraft Grated Parmesan Cheese* in the green metallic tube poured on a heap of angel hair pasta, the lights turned dim, and Laverne's loosely tied neckerchiefs...

Laurie Anderson... imagine an elf who lives in a tree-boll beside a volcano. Imagine an elf programming data sets, wrestling Andy Kaufman, retelling American history, wearing a silver lamay suit, surrounded by dancers in potato sack masks, playing loops of her own hypnotic voice with electric violin. Concurrent to New York's punk and no-wave scenes, Anderson rose to prominence in academic settings. Artist-in-residence at NASA. Bard with a mathematician's soul. Explorer of loss. Entity who would eventually fuse with Lou Reed.

Veruschka... with Penelope Tree as a close second, Veruschka was the ultimate avant-garde 60's supermodel, an air of chaos evident in her manifestations. She might appear as Artemis or a Zebra or in noir drag, tux and tails. She painted her body as a pile of bricks. She was a mantis hidden by twigs. Her severe Germanic face, limbs occupying the lens like those of a running gazelle.

Marilyn Monroe... screen icon of the Fifties, magnetic actress and comedienne who wanted to be taken seriously while pouting like a babydoll; died under mysterious circumstances after having affairs with the two most popular American politicians of the early Sixties who were on more kill lists than one can keep track of, including but not limited to the CIA.

Charlton Heston... a man with a face like a cinder block and a perpetually oiled chest. Often cast as a centurion or a lone human survivor of a depopulated world. Wholesome, ruthless, as American as a grilled cheese sandwich dipped in lead.

Dorothy Hamill... a woman with hair in the shape of a mushroom. She was an ice skater, but I think that anyone who lived through the decade of the Seventies will mainly remember the millions of young women who would go into beauty salons and request a "Dorothy Hamill" be done to their long and medieval locks, so that they, too, could be relieved of their burdens of personal chaos by having hair shaped like a mushroom.

White Russians... the first concoction I really got into as an adult drinker (not to be confused with the wine, rum-and-cokes or *Keystone* beer shared in the foot-smelling dorm rooms of metalheads (including one legally named *Prong*) or *Long Island Ice Teas* consumed with my *preferred* tribe of misfits (when I was seventeen)—drag queens.

California, a far west territory... barbarically stolen from the First Peoples, where melons, avocados, and silent films about Rasputin and the Sheik of Araby were produced to feed a novelty-starved public. Cast into severe drought; forest fires eclipsed by the strutting of Surfer Girls, Guatemalan turf-lords; setting for tech billionaires plotting world domination, and the susurrations of elderly Vietnam vets cohabiting the woods with next-level tweakers who quilt wizards' capes for raccoons.

Tigers... once roamed the Earth, were revered as gods, as masters of creation, hunted by the Industrial Ones as wall decorations and fertility charms, blown up with dynamite at the edge of tea plantations.

Joan Rivers... Comedienne and Gay Icon, martyred on the operating table after an anesthesia mishap. A petite snow-blonde battleship who hosted talk shows, advocated for the gender-transcendent costume experimentation of Leigh Bowery and a host of club kids, toured like clockwork, satirizing subjects as prosaic as marriage and as rarefied as the surgery she was addicted to. Famously said, "Beauty costs."

Rabbits... I really want rabbits, and willows, and koalas, and penguins, and bees and salamanders to survive...I get caught off guard and have *feelings* for them.

Mad Scientists... a confederation of misanthropes and Manifest Destiny apologists who suspect that biological life is an infestation, a sculpting paste too often past its prime; that a better world will be found by observing the behavior of drowning rats and the mass-production of cyanide bombs.

You Only Bend Once with a Spoonful of Mercury... arrived in a dream, the last words I heard before waking.

Fame... to show them, *really* show them. Success is the sweetest revenge even if the drive for it eats you like a cancer and you won't even *feel* it when you *have* it because it's the jungle-gym all over again and you're *Jenny Monster-Face* swinging across the bars and the boys are on top, perched like chimpanzees, punching your knuckles and hoping to make you fall, and the ground is so far away but you don't fall because you're going to *show* them, *as a girl* and *as an entity,* no one can take you down...oh no, three years have passed and where's your *new release?* Don't fall; you can't afford to fall...*yet*...it takes a lot of *work* to make your life appear to be more profound than other peoples', so much so that songs will be sung about your beauty and complete strangers will roll with a howling loneliness atop your grave because they were, by a tragic fluke of planetary rotation, born thirty-two years past your expiry.

The Future... but what does this matter *now,* oh, my apocalypse-pups? I whisper to you of vain endeavors; of beasts who wanted their names to last a thousand years, who wanted to rewrite genes and own oceans and have the perfect thigh-gap; they seethe in my subliminal life. And this *book,* I will be lucky if even *one* copy has made it to the tree-fort or underground commune where you squat fifteen years to this day, when there are so *few* of us left, and everything that happened before The Change, before you were born, might as well be a *dream.* Oh, desert devils, my airlock children...I wonder, when all I know is extinct, what manner of stories you will tell each other, what manner of future-dreams...

Jennifer Robin, November 2021

Now that didn't really clear things up, *did* it?

Also Out On Far West

farwestpress.com

+1 541-FAR-WEST

CPSIA information can be obtained
at www.ICGtesting.com
Printed in the USA
JSHW031914110222
22660JS00003B/9